FANCY ENGLISH
精湛英文

謝文欽 著

To have another language is to possess a second soul.

——Charlemagne

學習一種語言就像擁有一個新的靈魂，它能夠讓
你更深入地理解不同文化和思維。

——中世紀法蘭克王國查理曼大帝

作者序及導讀

學習英文是一件終身大事，對某些人而言更是興趣或者是工作上必備的能力，隨著時代潮流的推移，語言也不斷的更新，中、英文說法、用法都有所有精進與更新，作者我特別以這本書來「銜接」語言與人類文明演進的趨勢潮流，要您的英文實力輕鬆大躍進。

本書獨特之處在於以迅速、效率的方式，讓您沉浸在英文之中，不但擁有「Fancy English｜精湛英語」，更是可以讓你喜歡英文，說文解字，從結合時事、報導、短文文章、短文中，深入淺出的學習英文及實例的英文應用，瞭解每個字詞奧妙，搭配相關單字詞彙詞義，旁徵博引，讓學習更全面，讓學習的興趣更高，透過不斷的旁徵博引、旁敲側擊及演練，對於喜歡英文學習你絕對不能錯過這本，對提高學習興趣及實力有事半功倍，帶來耳目一新感覺的「Fancy English｜精湛英文」！

內容豐富多樣、包羅萬象，現代英文必須具備的知識，包括現代流行用語及詞彙的介紹，像是：同溫層Echo chamber、放鴿子Flake on、打混Dawdle、搭訕Accost、躺平Lie flat、擺爛Slack off、偷懶Veg out，電影上常常聽到的對白Don't patronize me.，社會問題常方面常會遇到像是作文需要使用的：厭女Misogyny、少子化Declining birthrate、高齡化Aging population、娘娘腔Sissy、中性性格Ambivert等的介紹；在法律上層面專用詞「補償、教唆、傳喚、潛逃、解除、失效、廢止、剝奪選舉權及心虛」的英文介紹及認識；在政治上：雙面人Duplicity、揭發Debunk、酸民、網軍、側翼、內幕、鬧劇一場……各種實用經典英文及應用；職業場上：倦怠Lethargy、Don't fob me off.不要敷衍我；口頭用語：電腦很卡My laptop is lacky、Don't patronize me；自然災害Deluge、Inundation、Calamity應用、金融企業專業用語包括：撤資Divest、破產Insolvent、債務違約Default on等實用有趣實用最新的介紹不一而足，還有更多華麗精湛必須知道的英文像是：黯然失色Pale by comparison、引人矚目Flamboyant、平凡無聊Mundane、活力充沛Ebullient，難以言諭Ineffable、無關緊要Nugatory、沆瀣一氣In cahoots、瑕不掩瑜、感同身受、活力充沛、輕而易舉……等英文的用語、替代的說法、文字探討及適用，這本書的誕生不但可以當成考試增進實力用書，更是喜愛英文，平時喜愛培養英文閱讀興趣的最佳夥伴，一定能讓您的學習更加精彩。

最新的AI人工智慧專文、糖尿病介紹、米其林美食及遊記的英文文章，更可以讓自己的英文單字庫豐富，更可以磨練實力及培養閱讀能力。總之這本書包羅萬象是現代最新的英文聖品，相信一定能為你帶來活力充沛的學習之旅，期待您的支持。

送給喜歡這本書的你

I want to share the following quotes with you,
someone who loves this book!
Life is a song - sing it.
Life is a game - play it.
Life is a challenge - meet it.
Life is a dream - realize it.
Life is a sacrifice - offer it.
Life is love - enjoy it.

目錄

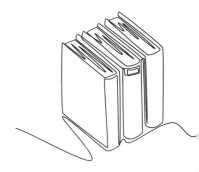

Abet | 教唆

Abet是一個動詞，指教唆、故意幫助、鼓勵或支持他人進行非法、不道德或錯誤的行為。而Abetment則是Abet的名詞形式，用來表示這種幫助或支持的行為。這兩個詞都在法律領域中經常使用，特別是在訴訟中追究協助犯罪者責任的情境下。

先來閱讀一下關於教唆Abet這個單字的解釋及短文：

Abet is a legal term in the continental legal system, referring to a criminal who intentionally incites another person to commit a crime. The perpetrator imparts their criminal intent to someone who either didn't have the intention to commit the crime or had wavering intent, thereby encouraging them to carry out the instructed crime. This act is known as abetment.

Abet教唆是大陸法系的法律術語，指的是一個犯罪分子故意煽動另一個人犯罪的行為。犯罪者將他們的犯罪意圖灌輸給原本沒有犯罪意圖或意圖不堅定的人，藉此鼓勵他們執行所指示的犯罪行為。這種行為稱為教唆。

Abet及Abetment的英文例句

1. The news report about a former basketball coach abetting the expenditure to incite threats and vandalize a female journalist's car is truly shocking. 一則有關一名前籃球教練協助支付資

金以煽動威脅並破壞一名女記者汽車的新聞報導確實令人震驚。

2. He was arrested for abetting the thieves by providing them with information about the security system. 他因向竊賊提供有關安全系統的訊息而被逮捕。

3. She was charged with abetment in the embezzlement scheme, as she knowingly helped the dishonest accountant hide the missing funds. 她被以教唆挪用公款起訴，因為她故意協助不誠實的會計人員藏匿遺失的資金。

4. The law prohibits abetment of any criminal activity, making it illegal to assist or encourage unlawful actions. 法律禁止幫助任何犯罪行為，使協助或鼓勵非法行為成為非法。

要注意的是Instigate和Abet在某些情境下可以被認為是意思相近的詞語，因為它們都涉及到在某個行為或事件中起到激勵、鼓動、或支持的作用。然而仍有些不同之處：

Instigate（煽動、激勵）
通常指引導或鼓動他人去開始某個行動、事件或不良行為，可能帶有負面或不道德的涵義。

He instigated the protest by making provocative statements. 他通過發表挑釁性的言論煽動了抗議活動。

Abet（教唆、支持、協助）
通常指在某個不當或非法的行動中提供支持、幫助、或鼓勵，可能是犯罪行為的共犯。

She was charged with abetting the robbery. 她被以教唆（幫助）搶劫起訴。

雖然這兩個詞在某些情境下可能表現出相似的含義，但它們的用法和語義上仍存在一些微妙的差異。

Instigate的同義詞，以及說明和例句

1. Incite（煽動）：指引導或激勵他人採取不好的行動。
   The provocative speech incited the crowd to violence. 挑釁性的演講煽動了人群進行暴力行為。

2. Provoke（挑釁）：意味著激怒或引起情感反應。
   Her comments provoked a heated debate. 她的評論引起了激烈的辯論。

3. Stir up（煽動）：意味著引起騷動或激起情感，常常用於描述引起困擾或混亂。
   The rumors stirred up panic among the residents. 謠言激起了居民的恐慌。

4. Evoke（喚起）：意味著喚起情感、回憶或反應，通常是不故意的。
   The painting evoked a sense of nostalgia. 這幅畫喚起了一種懷舊的情感。

5. Prompt（激勵）：意味著鼓勵或激發行動或思考。
   His success prompted others to follow his lead. 他的成功激勵了其他人效仿他的榜樣。

6. Encourage（鼓勵）：意味著提供支持或鼓勵，使某人有信心去做某事。

She encouraged him to pursue his dreams. 她鼓勵他追求自己的夢想。

7. Urge（敦促）：意味著強烈地要求或鼓勵某人做某事。

I urge you to reconsider your decision. 我敦促你重新考慮你的決定。

Abscond | 潛逃

Abscond是動詞，英文解釋：leave hurriedly and secretly, typically to avoid detection of or arrest for an unlawful action such as theft. 也就是逃走、潛逃躲藏。指突然離開或逃離某個地方，通常是爲了逃避法律追捕或避免責任。

我們來看幾個例子的實際應用

1. The news report reveals that a veteran Taiwanese actress is suspected of defrauding 2 million and, due to her absence from a court summons, has been absconded by the police. She has also fled the country and is now wanted for 15 years, leading to her mysterious disappearance from the entertainment industry. 新聞報導了一位台灣資深女星涉嫌詐欺200萬元，由於缺席法院傳喚，被警方指控爲「逃亡」。她也因此潛逃出境，遭到通緝15年，導致她神祕地從演藝圈消失。

2. The thief absconded from the scene of the crime before the police arrived. 小偷在警察抵達現場之前逃離了犯罪現場。

3. The company's CEO absconded with millions of dollars, leaving the employees and investors in shock. 公司的CEO帶走了數百萬美元，讓員工和投資者大爲震驚。

4. The prisoner managed to abscond from the prison by digging a tunnel over several months. 這名囚犯成功地在幾個月內挖了一條地道，逃離了監獄。

Abscond同義字，以及相應的英文造句

1. Flee逃離

   The suspect decided to flee the country to avoid arrest. 嫌疑犯決定逃離國家以避免被逮捕。

2. Escape逃離

   The prisoner managed to escape from his cell during the night. 囚犯在夜間成功逃離了牢房。

3. Bolt 狂奔／快閃

   When the fire alarm rang, the students bolted from the classroom. 當火警響起時，學生們從教室裡狂奔出來。

4. Absquatulate悄悄離開／溜走

   In the chaos, the treasure hunters decided to absquatulate with their findings. 在混亂中，尋寶者們決定帶著他們的發現物悄悄離開。

5. Make a getaway 逃離

   The bank robbers made a getaway in a stolen car. 銀行搶匪們在一輛偷來的汽車中逃跑了。

這些單字有時會根據上下文略有不同的用法，但都表示逃跑或逃離的意思。

Abstruse ｜ 艱澀難懂

Abstruse是形容詞，用來描述那些難以理解、晦澀或過於複雜的事物。通常在討論抽象或專業性的主題時使用，用來強調其難以理解的性質。

來看一下Abstruse在司法改革報導的文章之中如何運用？
Judicial rulings are often abstruse and hard to comprehend, leaving parties involved bewildered. Since the Judicial Reform National Conference last year, the Supreme Court has been actively promoting plain-language judgments. They have recently completed the development of a judgment editing system that can automatically identify archaic language in legal documents.
司法判決書用詞艱澀難懂，常讓當事人摸不到頭緒，司法院自去年司改國是會議後，開始推行判決書白話文，目前已經完成裁判書編輯系統功能，能夠自動識別文言文。

Abstruse的例句應用如下

1. The philosopher's writings are so abstruse that even scholars in the field struggle to decipher their meaning. 這位哲學家的著作如此晦澀，以至於即使是這個領域的學者也難以解讀它們的意思。

2. The manual for the advanced computer software was filled with abstruse technical jargon that left most users bewildered.

這款高階電腦軟體的手冊充滿了晦澀的技術術語，讓大多數使用者感到困惑。（註：Jargon指的是特定行業、專業領域或社群中使用的特殊術語、專業術語或隱語。這些術語對於非該領域的人是不容易理解的，因爲具有特定的含義或用法，可能與一般用語不同。通常在專業討論。）

3. The professor's lecture on quantum mechanics was so abstruse that only a few students managed to grasp the complex concepts.這位教授關於量子力學的講座如此晦澀，只有少數學生能夠掌握這些複雜的概念。

Abstruse的同義字

1. Obscure（模糊的）：難以理解或不容易被理解的事物。
   The professor's lecture on quantum physics was so obscure that most students struggled to grasp the concepts. 教授有關量子物理學的講座非常模糊，大多數學生難以理解其中的概念。

2. Cryptic（神祕的）：含有隱藏或祕密意義，需要解釋或解讀。
   The message he left was so cryptic that no one could figure out what he meant. 他留下的訊息非常神祕，沒有人能弄清楚他的意思。

3. Esoteric（深奧的）：僅供一小部分人理解或具有特殊知識的事物。
   Her interest in esoteric philosophies led her to explore ancient texts that most people had never heard of. 她對深奧的哲

學感興趣，因此她探索了大多數人從未聽說過的古代文獻。

4. Enigmatic（謎樣的）：令人困惑或難以理解的人事物。

The enigmatic smile on her face left everyone wondering what she was thinking. 她臉上的謎樣微笑讓每個人都想知道她在想什麼。

5. Abstruse形容某事物難以理解的詞語。

The novel's abstruse symbolism left literary critics debating its true meaning. 小說中深奧的象徵主義讓文學評論家們爭論其真正的含義。

值得說明的是，Profound深度的，是與Abstruse有相似之處的詞，但它們不完全相同。Profound指的是深刻的、有深度的，而不一定涉及難以理解或晦澀的概念。

The philosopher's speech on the meaning of life was truly profound and left the audience contemplating their existence. 哲學家有關生命意義的演講真的非常深刻，讓聽眾沉思自己的存在。

如你所見，profound在這個句子中指的是思想或概念的深度，而不是難以理解。與abstruse不同，profound可能是關於思想、感情或理解上的深度。

Accolade │ 榮譽／表彰

Accolade讚譽、榮譽。它是名詞，用來描述對某人或某事的高度讚揚、肯定或榮譽。

Accolade的例句

1. She received an accolade for her outstanding contribution to the field of science. 她因在科學領域的傑出貢獻而受到表彰。
2. The film received numerous accolades from critics and audiences alike. 這部電影獲得了評論家和觀眾的多次讚譽。
3. Winning the Nobel Prize is considered the highest accolade in the field of literature. 贏得諾貝爾獎被認為是文學領域中的最高榮譽。

Accolade的同義詞

1. Praise（名詞）：對某人或某事的讚美，表示肯定或欣賞。

   She received praise for her excellent performance in the play. 她因在劇中的優秀表現而受到讚美。
2. Honor（名詞）：尊敬或表彰，通常因為某人的卓越成就。

It was an honor to be awarded the Medal of Valor for his bravery. 被授予勇氣勳章是一種榮譽。

3. Commendation（名詞）：公開或正式的稱讚，表示認可。

The firefighter received a commendation for saving lives during the fire. 這名消防員因在火災期間拯救生命而受到表彰。

4. Recognition（名詞）：對某人或某事的認可或確認，通常是因爲他們的成就或貢獻。

Her research received international recognition for its groundbreaking discoveries. 她的研究因其開創性的發現而受到國際認可。

5. Applause（名詞）：大聲喝彩或鼓掌，表示對表演或演講的欣賞和支持。

The audience's applause echoed through the theater after the breathtaking performance. 令人驚嘆的表演結束後，觀衆的掌聲在劇院中回響。

這些詞彙在描述讚譽、肯定和榮譽時都可以使用，但仍應就上下文及語境考量文字的用法。

Accost｜搭訕

Accost動詞，主動接近或搭訕某人，通常是陌生人，可能是爲了交談、提問或尋求互動。

Me too自我保衛意識高漲，來看一下近期有一則新聞指出女性在捷運站出口附近被搭訕的報導，來了解一下Accost如何運用在文章中：

A female netizen posted a complaint, stating that she used to be able to stroll around Ximending（西門町）comfortably and freely. However, she doesn't know when it started, but she's often accosted by unfamiliar guys at the subway station exits. This is quite troublesome for her as an introverted person. After her post was exposed, it resonated with many female netizens.

一名女網友發文抱怨表示，以前她可以輕鬆自在地在西門町逛街，但不知從何時開始，她經常在捷運站出口被陌生男生搭訕，對內向的她來說十分困擾，貼文曝光後，引起許多女網友的共鳴。

Accost的應用例句

1. The stranger accosted me on the street and asked for directions. 陌生人在街上搭訕我，詢問路線。
2. She felt uncomfortable when a man accosted her in the park with intrusive questions. 當一名男子在公園裡用侵入性的

問題搭訕她時，她感到不舒服。

3. The journalist accosted the celebrity outside the restaurant to get an exclusive interview. 記者在餐廳外攔截了這位名人，以獲得一次獨家訪談。

Accost常用於描述一個人突然、直接地與另一個人交談，有時可能在對方未必願意的情況下。通常帶有一種主動的、有點冒昧的意味。

Accost的同義字

1. Approach走近，接近，通常是爲了交談或接觸他人。
   He decided to approach the stranger to ask for directions. 他決定走近那位陌生人詢問路線。

2. Confront面對，遭遇，通常指直接面對問題、困難或人。
   She had to confront her fear of public speaking to give the presentation. 她必須面對她對公開演說的恐懼才能進行簡報。

Importune、Solicit和Accost相似，都涉及到與他人進行互動及攀談，但在意義和用法上有所不同。

1. Accost走近，接近：通常是爲了交談或接觸他人，有時可能涉及對方不期望的方式。
   He accosted her on the street to ask for money. 他在街上走近她，要求借錢。

2. Importune強烈要求：尤其是一而再、煩人地要求某事，可能在對方不情願的情況下。

He continued to importune her for a date, even after she said no. 即使她拒絕了，他還在煩人地要求她約會。

3. Solicit尋求、請求：通常指正式地或禮貌地要求某事，例如幫助、建議、支持或資金。

She solicited donations for the charity event from local businesses. 她向當地企業正式請求捐款支持慈善活動。

Accost涉及走近和接觸，有時可能涉及不受歡迎的方式。Importune涉及強烈、煩人地要求。而solicit則是正式或禮貌地尋求某事，通常是在商業或正式情境中。

Acrid｜刺鼻

Acrid形容詞,刺鼻的、刺激性的。通常用來形容有害物質或氣味,具有強烈的、刺鼻的、不愉快的特徵。

之前台北捷運站發生旅客不小心按到防狼噴霧劑發出刺激性的味道的報導我們再看一下Acrid要怎麼運用在短文中:

In Taipei City, the subway police received a report about a passenger accidentally pressing the switch of a self-defense pepper spray canister inside their bag while searching for something. The pepper spray continued to discharge, filling the entire subway car with an acrid odor, causing quite a commotion. 北市捷運警察接獲報案,有民眾在翻找包包時,不慎按壓到包包內的防狼噴霧劑開關,防狼噴霧器不斷噴出,還伴隨著陣陣刺鼻惡臭瀰漫整個捷運車廂,引發不小波騷動。

來看一下應用例句及使用情境

1. The acrid smoke from the burning tires made it difficult to breathe. 刺鼻的輪胎燃燒煙霧讓呼吸變得困難。

2. The chemical spill in the lab released an acrid odor that forced everyone to evacuate. 實驗室的化學品洩漏釋放出一種刺鼻的氣味,迫使所有人撤離。

3. The acrid taste of spoiled milk was unmistakable, and he immediately spat it out. 腐壞牛奶的刺激性味道是無法搞錯

  FancyEnglish 精湛英文

的，他立刻把它吐了出來。

Acrid通常用來描述引起不適或不愉快感官體驗的情境，特別是與氣味或味道相關的。

以下為**Acrid**的同義字詞

1. Pungent（辛辣的）：指一種刺鼻或刺激的氣味，通常是因為化學物質或燃燒所產生的。

   The pungent smell of onions made my eyes water. 洋蔥的辛辣味讓我的眼睛流淚。

2. Sharp（刺鼻的）：用來形容氣味或味道，特別是當它們強烈且令人不快時。

   The sharp aroma of vinegar filled the kitchen. 醋的刺鼻香氣充滿了廚房。

3. Bitter（苦的）：當用來描述味道時，指的是一種令人不快的澀味或強烈的氣味。

   The bitter taste of the medicine was hard to swallow. 藥物的苦味很難咽下。

4. Caustic（腐蝕性的）：通常用來形容強烈而刺激性的氣味，有時帶有一種腐蝕性質。

   The caustic fumes from the chemical spill made it impossible to breathe. 來自化學品洩漏的腐蝕性煙霧讓人無法呼吸。

5. Noxious（有害的）：指對健康有害的氣味或物質，通常帶有強烈的不快感。

   The noxious fumes from the factory were a serious environmental concern. 工廠排放的有害煙霧是嚴重的環境問題。

Afflatus ｜ 靈感

靈感不是常常有的，台北捷運就有個特別的例子：Metro Taipei, drawing inspiration from creative afflatus, shared a Taipei Metro Food Map on Facebook, featuring the selected must-visit restaurants for this year, as recommended by Bib Gourmand.
台北捷運（Metro Taipei）發揮創意靈感，在臉書上分享了一份台北捷運美食地圖，展示了今年必比登所推薦的必訪餐廳。

Afflatus相似的同義字

Inspiration、Muse、Revelation、Eureka Moment（尤里卡效應 Eureka effect，也被稱爲：啊哈！時刻Aha! moment）都用來描述突然湧現的創意或靈感。

來看看二個例子

1. She felt a sudden afflatus and began to write a beautiful poem.
   她突然有了靈感，開始寫一首美麗的詩。
2. The afflatus of creativity struck him in the middle of the night. 創作的靈感在深夜襲來。

Aficionado │ 粉絲

Fan、Fanatic、Aficionado、Admirer、Enthusiast、Follower、Devotee等單字，都有一定程度上與粉絲相關，但它們有不同的意義和用法，我們來看一下實際的應用：

Media reports that Buffett, an aficionado of junk food, drinks five cans of cola every day, joking that it's his happiest hour, despite being willing to shorten his lifespan for junk food.

媒體報導，巴菲特是垃圾食品的愛好者，每天喝五罐可樂，開玩笑說這是他的最快樂時光，儘管他願意為垃圾食品縮短壽命。

其他與粉絲相關字詞舉例說明

1. Fanatic（狂熱者）：形容一個極度狂熱迷戀某事物的人，通常指的是對某個特定主題或活動過度熱衷的人。

   He's a fanatic when it comes to collecting vintage comic books. 他在收藏老式漫畫書方面是一個狂熱者。

2. Aficionado（狂熱愛好者）：形容對某項特定活動、主題或領域有深刻了解和濃厚興趣的人。

   She's a wine aficionado who can identify different types of wine blindfolded. 她是一位葡萄酒狂熱愛好者，能夠蒙住眼睛辨識不同種類的葡萄酒。

3. Devotee（愛好者）：指對某個特定事物或活動有忠誠和熱愛的人。

She's a devotee of classical music and attends every symphony concert in town. 她是古典音樂的愛好者，參加城裡每場交響樂音樂會。

4. Follower（追隨者）：在社交媒體上關注某個人、品牌或主題的人。

His Instagram has thousands of followers who admire his photography skills. 他的Instagram有成千上萬的追隨者，欣賞他的攝影技巧。

5. Enthusiast（熱衷者）：表示對某事物有極大的興趣和熱情。

He is an aviation enthusiast who collects model airplanes and studies aircraft history. 他是一位航空熱衷者，收藏模型飛機並研究飛機歷史。

6. Admirer（崇拜者）：指對某人或某事有深深崇拜和欣賞的人。

She is an admirer of the famous author and has read all of his books. 她是那位著名作家的崇拜者，讀過他所有的書。

7. Fan（粉絲）：指對某個藝人、團體、運動隊或事物有喜好的人，但通常不帶有狂熱的程度。

She's a fan of that famous singer and has all of his albums. 她是那位著名歌手的粉絲，擁有他所有的專輯。

希望這些解釋和例句有幫助！不同的詞語有不同的強調和用法，所以根據上下文選擇正確的詞語是很重要的。

Agog | 渴望

Be agog to是「非常期待」或「迫不及待」地等待某事發生的意思。用於形容對某事非常興奮和渴望。

This celebrity is stepping into the world of art for the first time, and he's incredibly agog to share his prepared work with everyone after months of dedicated preparation with his team.
這位明星首度踏足藝術這個新領域,他表示跟團隊過去幾個月經已盡全力籌備,此刻「非常期待」和大家分享這次展出作品。

其他的應用例子

1. She was agog to see the famous artist's latest exhibition. 她迫不及待地想要看到那位著名藝術家的最新展覽。
2. The children were agog to open their presents on Christmas morning. 孩子們迫不及待地想在聖誕早上打開禮物。
3. The fans were agog to meet their favorite movie star at the premiere. 影迷們迫不及待地想在首映禮上見到他們最喜歡的影星。

另外,以下的片語Be eager to、Be curious to、Feel excited about、Eagerly anticipate、Impetuously waiting也有「迫不及待」類似效果。

同義的片語

1. Be eager to（渴望）

   She is eager to start her new job and make a positive impact on the company. 她渴望著開始她的新工作，並對能對公司有積極影響感到期待。

2. Be curious to（好奇）

   The students were curious to learn more about the mysterious creature they had discovered in the forest. 學生們對於他們在森林中發現的神祕生物感到好奇，想更多了解。

3. Feel excited about（對⋯感到興奮）

   We all feel excited about the upcoming vacation to the tropical island. 我們都對即將到來的熱帶島嶼度假感到興奮。

4. Eagerly anticipate（熱切期待）

   The fans eagerly anticipate the release of the artist's new album. 粉絲們熱切期待藝人新專輯的發行。

5. Impetuously waiting（急不可耐地等待）

   He was impetuously waiting for the results of his bar exam, hoping he had passed. 他焦急地等待律師考試的成績，希望他已經通過了。

Ambivalent vs Iffy
矛盾 vs 不確定

Ambivalent是形容詞，形容當人或情況有矛盾、猶豫不決的情感或態度時的狀態。通常用來描述對於某件事物或情況既有正面也有負面的感覺，難以做出明確判斷或選擇。

以下是例句及應用

1. She felt ambivalent about the upcoming promotion because it meant more money but also more stress. 她對即將到來的升遷感到矛盾，因為這意味著更多的錢，但也意味著更多的壓力。

2. Their decision to move to a different country left them ambivalent; they were excited about new opportunities but sad to leave their home behind. 他們決定搬到另一個國家，讓他們感到矛盾；他們對新機會感到興奮，但也因離開家而感到傷感。

3. His ambivalent feelings towards the movie were evident in his mixed review; he liked the acting but found the plot confusing. 他對這部電影的矛盾感情在他的評論中顯而易見；他喜歡演技，但覺得劇情令人困惑。

Ambivalent通常在描述人對於某個選擇、情況或主題有複雜或相互衝突的情感時使用。

Ambivalent的同義詞

1. Conflicted：形容人在情感或態度上感到矛盾，難以做出明確的選擇或決定。

   She felt conflicted about whether to accept the job offer in a different city or stay with her current company. 她對於是否接受在另一個城市的工作邀請或留在目前的公司感到矛盾。

2. Torn：形容人被不同的選擇或情感拉扯，很難做出決定。

   He was torn between spending the weekend with his family or attending the important conference for work. 他在是否與家人度過週末或參加重要的工作會議之間感到矛盾。

3. Mixed：形容情感或感覺有多種不同的元素或成分，包括正面和負面的。

   Her review of the restaurant was mixed; she loved the food but was disappointed by the service. 她對這家餐廳的評價是褒貶不一的；她喜歡食物，但對服務感到失望。

Ambivalent和Iffy都描述了對某事物或情況的不確定、矛盾或猶豫不決的感覺，但它們在強調方面有些不同

Ambivalent更強調兩種相反的情感或態度在同一時間存在，讓人難以做出明確的決定。

Iffy則更強調不確定性和不穩定性，暗示一些疑慮或不確定因素可能導致猶豫。

來看看以下的例句

1. She was ambivalent about whether to accept the job offer because it required her to move away from her family, but the salary was tempting. 她對於是否接受這份工作的決定感到矛盾，因為這需要她遠離家人，但薪水很誘人。

2. His performance in the interview was iffy; he had relevant experience, but his communication skills were not convincing. 他在面試中的表現令人懷疑；他有相關經驗，但他的溝通能力不夠令人信服。

Ambivalent較多強調矛盾的情感，而Iffy則偏向描述不確定性和可疑的情況。

Ambivert │ 中性性格的人

我們知道outgoing、extrovert、gregarious是指外向活潑的
（人）；內向害羞的（人）為introvert、timid、reclusive
individual。

你是內向還是外向的人呢？有一種「中性性格」指的是性格
特點沒有明顯偏外向積極、或悲觀內向。在英語中ambivert
就是指「中性性格」的人，可以用balanced personality或
moderate extrovert-introvert來描述類似的性格特點。這種中
性性格可能表現為冷靜、理性，不會極端地偏向某一方面。
當然每個人的性格都是獨特的，中性性格只是性格的一種可
能特徵，而不是絕對的分類。

Ambivert的例句及應用

1. As an ambivert, Mark can adapt to any situation, whether it's
   a lively party or a peaceful afternoon of introspection. 馬克是
   一個中性性格的人，他可以適應任何情境，不論是熱鬧
   的派對還是寧靜的午後自省。

2. Being an ambivert, Alex finds balance in life by alternating
   between energetic outdoor adventures and cozy indoor nights
   with Netflix. 亞歷克斯因為屬於中性性格特質的人，在
   生活中能夠在充滿活力的戶外冒險和舒適的在房間欣賞
   Netflix間找到平衡。

Angst │ 焦慮

Angst是名詞，指一種深切的焦慮、不安或內心的痛苦感。通常用來描述一種情感狀態，特別是與個人的存在、生活意義或社會問題相關的焦慮感。

Angst例句的運用

1. The impending exams filled her with a sense of deep angst. 即將來臨的考試讓她充滿了深刻的焦慮感。

2. He often experienced existential angst, questioning the purpose of life. 他經常感到存在的焦慮，質疑生活的目的。

3. The film portrayed the protagonist's inner angst as he struggled with his past mistakes. 電影呈現了主角內心的痛苦感，因為他在努力應對自己過去的錯誤。

Angst通常用來描述一種情緒或內心的掙扎，特別是當人感到不確定、困惑或無法應對某些重要問題時。強調一種內在的情感困惑或焦慮，而不僅僅是一般的擔憂。

與Angst類似的同義詞

1. Anxiety：指一種對未來或不確定性的強烈擔憂感。

   Her anxiety about the job interview made it hard for her to sleep. 她對工作面試的焦慮讓她難以入睡。

2. Dread：表示對某事的強烈害怕或不安。

He had a sense of dread before confronting his fears. 在面對自己的恐懼之前，他有一種害怕感。

3. Worry：指對一個或多個問題的長時間擔心或焦慮。

She couldn't stop worrying about her sick grandmother. 她無法停止擔心她生病的祖母。

4. Apprehension：意味著對未來事件的擔憂或不安，有一些基礎的擔心。

His apprehension about the upcoming exam was evident in his behavior. 他對即將來臨的考試的擔憂在他的行為中表現得很明顯。

5. Unease：輕微但持續的不安或焦慮感。

There was an unease in the room as they waited for the verdict. 當他們等待判決時，房間裡充滿了不安。

以上都可以用來描述對未來、不確定性或困難情況的心理狀態，但它們在細微的情感差異上可能有所不同。Angst通常指的是一種深切的、內在焦慮或內心痛苦感。

Apotheosis │ 巔峰

Apotheosis神化、封神、巔峰，指一個人或事物已提升到神聖或巔峰的地位。

In her 30th year in the industry, 李玟（Coco Lee）achieved the apotheosis of her career, not only becoming a household name in the Chinese music scene but also becoming the first Asian singer to perform at the Oscars awards ceremony.
李玟出道第30年，事業達到巔峰，除了紅遍華人樂壇，更是首位在奧斯卡頒獎典禮演唱的亞洲歌手。

與Apotheosis相關的同義詞

culmination頂點、climax高潮、peak高峰、apex頂點、zenith頂點、deification神化、divinization神化、exaltation崇高、sublimation昇華、transcendence超越、sanctification神聖化、epicenes。這些詞彙都表達了某人或某事物提成就已達巔峰或神聖的狀態的概念。如何使用取決於具體的上下文情境。

同義單字的例句

1. Culmination（頂點）：在一系列事件或過程中的最高點。

   Winning the championship was the culmination of years of hard work and dedication. 贏得冠軍是多年來辛勤工作和奉

獻的頂點。

2. Climax（高潮）：故事或事件的最高點，最令人興奮的部分。

The movie's climax had the audience on the edge of their seats. 電影的高潮部分讓觀眾坐立難安。

3. Peak（高峰）：指最高點或最強烈的時刻。

Hiking to the peak of the mountain was a challenging but rewarding experience. 爬上山頂是一次具有挑戰性但令人滿足的經歷。

4. Apex（頂點）：表示最高或最重要的點或事物。

His performance reached its apex during the final act of the play. 他的表現在劇的最後一幕達到了巔峰。

5. Zenith（頂點）：表示事物的最高或最頂級的狀態。

Her career was at its zenith when she won the prestigious award. 她的職業生涯在她贏得了這個重要獎項時達到了巔峰。

6. Deification（神化）

The hero's deeds led to his deification among the people. 英雄的事蹟使他在民眾中神化。

7. Exaltation（崇高）

The singer's performance brought an exaltation of emotions to the audience. 歌手的表演讓觀眾情感高昂。

8. Transcendence（超越）

The artist's work achieved a level of transcendence that left everyone in awe. 藝術家的作品達到了一種超越的境界，讓所有人感到敬畏。

9. Epicness（史詩級）

Example: The battle scenes in the movie were filled with epicness and grandeur. 電影中的戰鬥場面充滿史詩般的壯麗。

10. Supremacy（至高）

The company's technological innovations solidified its supremacy in the industry. 該公司的技術創新鞏固了它在行業中的至上地位。

11. Pinnacle（巔峰）

Winning the championship was the pinnacle of his athletic career. 贏得冠軍是他運動生涯的巔峰。

12. Culmination（高峰）

The fireworks show was the culmination of the week-long festival. 煙火表演是為期一週節慶的頂峰。

希望這些同義字及例句能夠幫助更好地理解和使用 Apotheosis。

Artificial intelligence
｜人工智慧

先討論一下幾個重要的單字：Congruous、Gen AI、Ubiquitous、Be incumbent upon、Profound and prudent impact、Elusive。

1. Congruous（一致的，相符的），同義字有Compatible、Harmonious、Corresponding。

2. Gen AI（生成式AI）、深度學習Deep learning、機器學習Machine learning：

   （1）機器學習是一種AI透過模型從大數據中學習模式、趨勢和關聯性，並以參數調整來強化產出預測及決策的性能；

   （2）生成式AI如生成對抗網絡（GANs）或序列到序列模型，來創建新數據；

   （3）深度學習Deep Learning則是使用深度神經網絡來解決各種包括圖像識別、語音識別、自然語言處理等問題。

3. Ubiquitous（無所不在的，普遍存在的）：Pervasive、Omnipresent、Ever-Present也有類似意思。

4. Be incumbent upon（是……的責任，義不容辭）Be obligatory、Be required、Be one's duty。像例句：It is incumbent upon us to protect the environment for future generations.保護環境是我們對後代的責任。

5. Profound and Prudent Impact（深遠而謹慎的影響）

6. Elusive（難以捉摸的），同義詞Evasive、Slippery、Hard to grasp、intangible、evanescent。例句The solution to the room-temperature superconductor remained elusive despite extensive research. 儘管進行了大量研究，但常溫超導體的解決方案仍然難以理解／掌握／捉摸。

一起來閱讀及欣賞這篇精彩的人工智慧AI有關文章吧！

The rapid and congruous development of artificial intelligence, especially Gen Ai、Deep Learning & Machine Learning, is gradually becoming a ubiquitous and consistent force, profoundly influencing our future. As this evolution of AI continues to accelerate, discussions regarding its future prevalence are intensifying. It is incumbent upon us as humanity to reflect on the profound and prudent impact of AI on legal frameworks.

人工智慧的迅速而協調的發展，特別是生成式AI、深度學習和機器學習，正無處不在且持續深刻地影響著我們的未來。隨著AI的演進不斷加速，關於其未來普及的討論也日益激烈。作為人類，我們有責任思考AI法律的框架，及其深遠和謹慎影響。

Recently, international consensus on the governance of AI remains elusive, with countries like Japan, the United Kingdom, and the United States temporarily refraining from legislation to avoid stifling innovation. Taiwan also leans towards not constraining the development of AI. The government is inclined to formulate a Basic Law on Artificial Intelligence, with a focus on cautious governance that strikes a harmonious balance between risk reduction and fostering development.

最近，國際社會在人工智慧的治理方面尚未達成共識，日本、英國和美國等國暫時避免立法以避免扼殺AI的創新。台灣也傾向於不限制AI的發展。政府傾向於制定人工智慧基本法，重點是謹慎的治理，以在風險減少和促進發展之間找到平衡。

Ballyhoo｜大肆宣傳

Ballyhoo可當名詞和動詞，用來形容誇張或大肆宣傳某事物，伴隨著喧鬧和吵鬧。可以指喧囂的廣告、誇張的宣傳、或對某事物的過度吹捧。

我們來看一則蘋果公司最近在接受記者詢問有關〈蘋果公司為何沒有針對AI投資大肆宣傳？〉的一篇報導：

In contrast to other tech giants, Apple has refrained from excessive ballyhoo regarding its investments in Artificial Intelligence（AI）. Tim Cook stated, We view AI and machine learning as fundamental core technologies integrated into nearly all our products. He emphasized that AI is not only applied to recent software features like the announced voice mailbox but also to existing functionalities like car crash detection or fall detection. Apple has been researching AI technology in various domains for years, including generative AI, and intends to continue its research in the future.

與其他科技巨頭不同，蘋果一直避免大肆宣傳其在人工智慧（AI）方面的投資。庫克表示：「我們將AI和機器學習視爲幾乎融入我們所有產品的基本核心技術。」他強調，AI不僅應用於最新的軟體功能，如宣布的語音信箱，還應用於現有功能，如車禍檢測或跌倒檢測。蘋果多年來一直在各個領域研究AI技術，包括生成式AI，並計劃在未來繼續進行研究。

來看一下應用**Ballyhoo**的例句

1. The new product launch was accompanied by a lot of ballyhoo in the media. 新產品的推出伴隨著媒體上的大肆宣傳。

2. The restaurant's ballyhoo about having the world's best burger turned out to be just hype. 這家餐廳關於擁有「世界上最好的漢堡」的宣傳，事實證明只是為了炒作而已。

3. Despite all the ballyhoo surrounding the movie, some viewers found it disappointing. 儘管電影受到了大肆宣傳，但有些觀眾覺得它令人失望。

Ballyhoo的同義詞及意思

1. Hype（炒作、大肆宣傳）：對某事物過度宣傳或誇大其價值的行為。

   The company's marketing team created a lot of hype around their new product. 公司的營銷團隊對他們的新產品進行了大肆宣傳。

2. Puffery（誇大宣傳）：指有意誇大事物的好處或價值，通常用於推銷產品或服務。

   The advertisement was full of puffery, making it hard to trust the claims. 廣告充滿了誇大宣傳，讓人難以相信這些聲稱。

3. Exaggeration（誇大）：指對某事物或情況的誇張描述，通常用於引起注意或吸引更多關注。

   His story was filled with exaggerations, making it difficult to separate fact from fiction. 他的故事充滿了誇大之詞，讓人難以將事實和虛構區分開來。

4. Promotion（促銷、宣傳）：指推廣產品、服務或活動的行為，通常以吸引更多人的注意。

The promotion of the concert involved a lot of marketing and advertising. 音樂會的宣傳包括了大量的營銷和廣告。

Banter | 有說有笑

Banter名詞，也可以用作動詞，輕鬆、幽默且友好的交談或玩笑話。用來形容一種愉快的互動，其中人們以幽默的方式互相嘲笑或調侃。在朋友、同事之間或在輕鬆的社交場合中使用。強調友好的氛圍，其中人們可以互相取笑，但這是出於友好和愉快的目的，而不是冒犯或傷害。

Banter的英文例句及應用

1. During the lunch break, there was a lot of banter among the coworkers as they teased each other about their favorite sports teams. 午休時間，同事之間相互嘲笑彼此喜愛的運動隊伍，引起了許多歡樂的言談。

2. Sarah and John enjoyed the playful banter in their relationship; it kept their conversations lively and fun. Sarah和John喜歡在他們的關係中進行愉快的調侃，這使得他們的對話充滿了活力和樂趣。

3. The banter between the comedians had the audience in stitches, with everyone laughing uncontrollably. 這兩位喜劇演員之間的調侃讓觀眾捧腹大笑，每個人都無法控制地笑倒。（註：had the audience in stitches是俚語表達，意思是某事或某人讓觀眾非常大笑，笑得無法自控。）

Banter的同義字

1. Chaff（戲弄）：Light-hearted teasing or joking. Chaff是指輕鬆、幽默或調侃性的言談，通常是友好的，旨在引起笑聲而不是傷害感情。

   They engaged in some friendly chaff about each other's sports teams. 他們開始對彼此的運動隊伍進行友好的戲弄。

2. Rally（嘲笑、奚落）：Playful and humorous exchange of remarks. 意指在互動中進行輕鬆、幽默的言詞交流，人們通常會互相開玩笑或取笑對方，但是這種交流是友好的。

   The comedian rallied the politician with jeers and insults. 喜劇演員用嘲笑和辱罵來奚落政客。

3. Badinage（戲言）：Light and playful conversation or banter. 意味著輕鬆、幽默的對話或言詞，常用於友好的、愉快的互動，目的是輕鬆地交流和取悅。

   Their badinage was filled with laughter and jests. 他們的戲言充滿了笑聲和笑話。

4. Raillery（嘲笑）：Good-natured teasing or mocking. Raillery 表示以友好和幽默的方式嘲笑或戲弄他人，通常是為了開玩笑而不是傷害感情。

   She responded to his raillery with a witty comeback. 她對他的嘲笑以機智的回應作答。

5. Teasing（取笑）：Making fun of someone or provoking them in a playful way. 意味著以友好或開玩笑的方式來取笑或戲弄某人，這種行為通常是無惡意的，目的是帶來歡笑。

The teasing among siblings was all in good fun.兄弟姐妹之間的戲弄都是出於開玩笑的。

  FancyEnglish 精湛英文

Beguile
| 欺騙／吸引及消磨時間

Beguile是很常閱讀到的字彙，但是這個單字有幾個不同的意思，容易混淆：

1. 欺騙：意指用詭計或花言巧語欺騙某人，尤其是誘使他們相信不實之事。

   He tried to beguile her into investing in a fraudulent scheme. 他試圖欺騙她投資一個詐騙計劃。

2. 吸引：表示吸引、迷惑或引誘某人，使他們感到愉悅或沉浸其中。

   The beautiful scenery of the countryside never fails to beguile tourists. 美麗的鄉村風光總是能吸引遊客。

3. 消磨時間：意味著用輕鬆愉快的方式度過時間，通常是在等待或無所事事的情況下。

   She beguiled the long hours of the train journey by reading a captivating novel. 她透過閱讀一本引人入勝的小說來消磨漫長的火車旅程的時間。

當涉及到Beguile不同意思時的一些同義詞及例句

1. Beguile「欺騙」解釋時同義詞：Deceive、Mislead、Cheat
   She tried to deceive her friend by pretending to be someone else on the phone. 她試圖通過假裝成別人打電話來欺騙她的朋友。

The salesman misled customers by promising features that the product didn't have. 那位銷售員通過承諾產品沒有的功能，誤導了顧客。

He cheated in the game by peeking at his opponent's cards. 他在遊戲中作弊，偷看對手的牌。

2. Beguile當「吸引」時同義詞：Entice、Charm、Captivate

The fragrance of fresh-baked bread enticed people into the bakery. 新鮮烤麵包的香氣吸引著人們走進了麵包店。

Her charming smile won over everyone at the party. 她迷人的微笑贏得了派對上所有人的喜愛。

The magician's performance captivated the audience with its stunning illusions. 魔術師的表演以令人驚嘆的幻覺迷住了觀眾。

3. Beguile當「消磨時間」解釋時同義詞：Pass（the）time、Amuse oneself、Kill time

He read a novel to pass the time while waiting for the delayed flight. 他讀了一本小說來打發等待航班延誤的時間。

The children amused themselves by playing in the park all afternoon. 孩子們整個下午都在公園裡玩耍，自得其樂。

We played card games to kill time during the long train journey. 長途火車旅行中，我們玩撲克牌來打發時間。

希望這些例句能幫助你更好地理解及運用Beguile及其相關意思同義單字的用法。

Binge ｜大胃王／購物狂

Binge當作為「名詞」

一陣狂熱或過度的行為，通常指飲食或消費方面的過度。當某人在短時間內大量進食或大量消費某物品時，通常在情感或壓力的影響下，可以使用。

當作為「動詞」

進行狂熱或過度的行為，通常指大量進食或大量消費某物品。描述某人在某個時間段內一直不斷進食或過度使用某物品，例如電視節目、網絡內容等，可以使用。

Binge及Binge-eating狂吃（的）的應用

1. He's a competitive eater, known for his binge-eating feats, and he holds several records for consuming massive amounts of food in a short time. 他是一位以狂吃食物而聞名的大胃王，並且在短時間內消耗大量食物方面擁有多個記錄。

2. She became a food challenge champion by binge-eating her way through the 10-pound burger challenge in under 20 minutes. 她通過在不到20分鐘內狂吃了10磅漢堡的方式成為了一名食品挑戰冠軍。

3. She went on a shopping binge last weekend and bought way more than she needed. 她上週末瘋狂購物，買了遠遠超過她需要的東西。

4. After a long week of work, he binged on his favorite TV series all night. 在一個辛苦的工作週之後，他整夜沉迷於他最喜歡的電視劇。

5. Binge-eating can be a response to stress or emotional distress for some individuals. 對於某些人來說，狂吃可能是對壓力或情感困擾的一種應對方式。

binge的同義詞及造句

1. Feast（盛宴）：大量進食或享受美食的行為。

   During the holiday season, many people indulge in a feast of delicious treats. 在假期季節，許多人沉迷於享受美味食物的盛宴。

2. Gorge（狂吃）：狂吃大量食物，通常是在短時間內。

   After the marathon, he gorged on pizza and ice cream to replenish his energy. 馬拉松賽後，他狂吃披薩和冰淇淋以補充能量。

3. Overindulge（過度沉溺）：過度沉溺於某種行為，通常是指飲食或享受娛樂。

   She tends to overindulge in online shopping when she's stressed. 當她感到壓力時，她傾向於過度沉溺於網上購物。

4. Pig out：放縱地大吃特吃。

   We decided to pig out on junk food while watching movies all night. 我們決定一整晚看電影時縱情大吃垃圾食品。

5. Devour（狼吞虎嚥）：狼吞虎嚥地吃，通常指快速吃完大量食物。

The hungry kids devoured the entire pizza within minutes. 餓極了的孩子們在幾分鐘內吃光了整個比薩。

6. Pound food：迅速且大量地吃食物。

After the race, he pounded food to refuel his exhausted body. 比賽後，他大口吃食物來恢復體力。

以上這些詞彙都用於描述過度進食或過度沉溺於某種行為的情境，請細細品味。

Brevity｜簡潔

Brevity意思是簡潔或簡練，用來表示訊息或表達方式非常簡單而且不冗長。通常用於強調言詞或文字的簡單和簡潔，以便更清楚地傳達訊息或思想。

來看一下Brevity例句的應用

1. His speech was known for its brevity; he could convey complex ideas in just a few words. 他的演講以言詞簡潔而聞名；他可以用很少的詞語傳達復雜的思想。

2. The brevity of the instructions made it easy for everyone to understand the process. 簡潔的指導使每個人都能容易理解這個過程。

Brevity的同義詞及例句

1. Conciseness（簡潔）：指言詞或文字的簡潔和明了。

   The conciseness of the report made it easy to understand. 報告的簡潔使其易於理解。

2. Succinctness（簡明）：表示以簡明扼要的方式表達，避免不必要的細節。

   Her succinctness in answering questions impressed the audience. 她在回答問題時的簡明印象深刻觀眾。

3. Briefness（簡短）：意指言詞或表達的短暫性質，不經過多的細節或冗長。

The briefness of his response left me with more questions. 他回答的簡短讓我有更多問題。

4. Terse（簡潔而含蓄）：描述一種簡練、簡潔但可能稍微含蓄的方式表達。

His terse email conveyed the urgency of the situation. 他簡短的電子郵件表達了情況的緊急性。

5. Economy of words（節省言詞）：指使用最少的詞語來傳達訊息或思想，以確保言詞的簡明。

She mastered the economy of words in her writing, conveying powerful messages with brevity. 她在寫作中掌握了語言的精隨，用簡潔的文字傳達強有力的訊息。

這些詞語都與brevity有關，表示言詞或表達方式的簡潔、簡明和精簡。

Brood｜陷入沉思

Brood作爲名詞

意指「一窩」（尤指家禽）的幼雛，通常是鳥類的幼鳥。

She found a brood of baby ducks in her backyard. 她在後院發現一窩小鴨子。

Brood作爲動詞

意指長時間憂慮、苦惱或思考某事，常常指消極或困擾的思考。Brood over就是這個動詞的短語形式：

He tends to brood over his past mistakes. 他經常沉思自己的過去錯誤。

He brooded over his need to find a wife. 他陷入對尋找妻子的需求的沉思之中。

和Brood over有關的詞彙

有Fret about煩惱、Mope about沮喪、Languish over憂鬱、Feel despondent about（對某事感到絕望）、Contemplate（思考）

例句和用法

1. Brood over（苦惱於）：指長時間思考、憂慮或困擾於某事情上。

    She tends to brood over her mistakes instead of moving on. 她經常苦惱於自己的錯誤，而不願意往前看。

2. Fret about（煩惱於）：表示因擔憂、不安或煩躁而感到不舒服。

Don't fret about the small stuff; it's not worth it. 別為小事煩惱，不值得的。

3. Mope about（沮喪於）：意味著情緒低落，通常表現為無精打采或消極的行為。

He's been moping about since he didn't get the job he wanted. 自從他沒有得到他想要的工作後，他一直感到沮喪。

4. Languish over（憂鬱於）：暗示因為長期忍受某種困境或困擾而感到痛苦。

She has been languishing over her failed relationship for months. 她因為失敗的戀情而委靡不振好幾個月了。

5. Feel despondent about（對……感到絕望）：表示因某種情況或事件而感到極度沮喪和失望。

After the loss, he felt despondent about the future. 在失去之後，他對未來感到絕望。

6. Contemplate（思考）：意味著深思熟慮或考慮某事，通常是一個想法或計劃。

She likes to contemplate the meaning of life when she's alone. 她喜歡在獨處時思考生命的意義。

Burst out | 哭得死去活來

Burst out crying和Burst into tears都用來描述突然、急切地開始哭泣或大哭的情況。它們通常用於表達情感烈、悲傷、失望、或高興等情況下的哭泣。

來看一段關於李玟遭霸凌，名人痛哭的文字，如何將這個片語應用在文章中：

In the midst of the controversy surrounding the talent show Chinese Good Voice, where leaked recordings appeared to bully the singer Coco Lee, many disturbing revelations have come to light. This has triggered an unprecedented public outcry, leading to the suspension of the show's broadcast. Celebrities who have been vocal in support of Coco Lee burst out crying upon hearing the news. They shared that Coco Lee had a dream just a few days ago and said, Tonight, she will come to thank everyone. Rest in peace, Coco!

在圍繞著選秀節目《中國好聲音》的爭議中，一些外洩的錄音似乎在霸凌歌手李玟（CoCo），曝光了許多令人不安的內幕。這引發了前所未有的大規模公憤，導致該節目的播出暫停。許多聲援李玟的名人在聽到這個消息時不禁痛哭失聲。他們分享李玟幾天前曾做過一個夢，並說：「今晚，她將前來感謝大家。CoCo，安息吧！」（註：Vocal是「聲音的」或「有聲的」。用來形容與聲音、歌唱或說話相關的事

物，如「vocal表演」指的是歌唱表演，或「vocal錄音」指的是聲音的錄音。此外，vocal也可以用來形容表達意見或意見強烈的人，表示他們在某個議題上非常直言不諱或積極參與。）

Burst out crying的例句

1. She couldn't contain her grief any longer and burst out of crying at the funeral. 她再也無法克制她的悲傷，在葬禮上大哭了出來。

2. When she heard the heartwarming surprise, she burst out crying with joy. 當她聽到令人感動的驚喜時，她高興得大哭了起來。

3. After the breakup, he burst out crying in front of his friends, unable to hold back his emotions. 分手後，他在朋友面前情不自禁地大哭起來。

Burst into tears的例句

1. The little girl burst into tears when she realized she had lost her favorite toy. 當小女孩意識到她弄丟了她最喜歡的玩具時，她哭了起來。

2. When he saw the injured puppy on the side of the road, he immediately burst into tears. 當他看到路邊受傷的小狗時，他立刻哭了出來。

3. Overwhelmed with gratitude, she burst into tears upon receiving the unexpected gift. 感激之情油然而生，她在收到這個意外的禮物時不禁哭了起來。

這兩個表達方式可以互換使用，描述了瞬間的情感爆發而引起的哭泣。

Burst out crying和Burst into tears的相關片語及例句

1. Start sobbing：意思是突然開始大聲哭泣，通常伴隨著淚水。

   When he heard the tragic news, he couldn't help but start sobbing. 當他聽到悲慘的消息時，他情不自禁地開始大聲哭泣。

2. Break down in tears：意思是情感崩潰，突然開始哭泣。

   She broke down in tears when she saw the damage to her car. 當她看到她的車受損時，她情緒崩潰，突然開始哭泣。

3. Burst into sobs：意思是突然大聲啜泣，通常表示情感極度激動。

   Overwhelmed by the surprise party, she burst into sobs of joy. 在驚喜派對的感動下，她情不自禁地大聲啜泣了起來。

4. Choke up：意思是因為情感而變得說不出話來，可能伴隨著哭泣。

   He choked up with gratitude when he received the award. 當他收到獎項時，他因感激而說不出話來。

這些詞語和片語都用於描述情感爆發，通常涉及大聲哭泣或情感崩潰的情境。它們可以依照情境及上下文互換使用。

Calamity｜重大災害

Calamity名詞，嚴重的災害、不幸事間或災害

President Biden declared the wildfires in Hawaii a calamity and released federal funds for the hard-hit area of Maui Island. 美國總統拜登宣布夏威夷州的野火是「重大災難」，爲重災區毛伊島釋出聯邦資金。

Calamitous形容詞，災難性的

The flood had calamitous consequences for the town's infrastructure. 洪水對該城市的基礎設施產生了災難性的後果。

Calamity的同義字詞如下

1. Disaster（災害）

   The earthquake was a disaster for the entire region. 這次地震整個地區來說都是一場災難。

2. Catastrophe（災難）

   The hurricane was a catastrophic event that caused widespread damage. 那場颶風是一場造成廣泛損害的災難事件。

3. Tragedy（悲劇）：

   The plane crash was a tragic event that took many lives. 那次飛失事是一起悲劇，奪去了許多人的生命。

4. Misfortune（不幸）：

Losing his job was a great misfortune for him and his family.
失業對他和他的家人來說是巨大的不幸。

★Scourge是造成社會重大災禍，例如人的行為造成的社會問題，健康、環境或道德方面的持續問題和困擾。像是毒品、貧窮或是假新聞造成的災禍，和災難calamity還是有所區別。

Scourge的英文例句及應用

1. Drug addiction is a scourge that affects communities worldwide. 毒品成癮是一影響全球社區的災禍。
2. Poverty is a scourge that afflicts many developing nations. 貧困是困擾許多發展中國家的禍根。
3. The opioid epidemic has become a scourge in many communities across the United States. 鴉片類藥物濫用成癮已經成為美國許多社區的禍害。
4. Corruption is a scourge that undermines the trust of citizens in their government. 貪污是一種動搖公民對政府信任的禍端。
5. The spread of fake news has become a scourge of the digital age. 假新聞的傳播已成為數位時代的災難。

Callous | 冷酷無情

Callous是形容詞，他的名詞是callousness表示一種冷酷、無情或無感情的特質，通常指某人對他人的感受或需求缺乏關懷或同情。都市步調快速，人與人的距離也變遠，不過若有需要幫助時，相信仍有許多人願意伸出援手。

不久之前有則報導，一名網友以「台北人的冷漠總是令人驚訝」為題，指年輕人搭車沒有讓座給老人家，讓他感到難過。不過，貼文一出馬上遭網友批評「憑什麼要道德綁架？」我們來看如何應用Callousness這個單字到文章之中：

In the fast-paced urban environment, distances between people have grown, but when help is needed, there's still a belief that many are willing to lend a hand. Recently, a netizen posted under the title The Callousness of Taipei Residents Always Surprises Me, pointing out that young people on public transportation didn't offer their seats to the elderly, which made him feel sad. However, the moment the post went up, it was immediately criticized by other netizens who questioned, Why should we be subjected to moral coercion?

在快節奏的城市環境中，人與人之間的距離變得遙遠，但在需要幫助的時候，人們仍然相信許多人願意伸出援手。最近，一位網友在標題為「台北居民的冷漠總是讓我感到驚訝」的帖子下發文，指出在公共交通工具上，年輕人沒有讓座給年長者，這讓他感到難過。然而，一發布立刻遭到其他

網友的批評，他們質疑：「爲什麼我們應該受到道德的強制呢？」

Callous的英文的應用例句

1. His callous response to her suffering shocked everyone in the room. 他對她的痛苦作出的冷酷回應令房間內的每個人都感到震驚。

2. The manager's callous decision to lay off employees without notice angered the staff. 經理冷酷地決定在不提前通知的情況下裁員，激怒了員工。

3. The defendant's callous disregard for the victim's pain was evident during the 被告對受害者的痛苦漠不關心，在審判過程中顯而易見。

Callous的同義詞以及例句

1. Heartless（冷酷）：指對他人的感受或需求缺乏同情心，類似於callous。

   His heartless actions left the family in despair. 他的無情行爲讓這個家庭感到絕望。

2. Unfeeling（無感情）：表示缺乏情感或共鳴，通常指在關鍵時刻表現冷漠。

   She was unfeeling when her friend needed support. 當她的朋友需要支持時，她表現得無情。

3. Insensitive（不敏感）：指對他人的情感或需要缺乏敏感度，可能是因爲缺乏意識或關心。

   His insensitive remarks hurt her deeply. 他不敏感的言論深

深傷害了她。

4. Cold-hearted（冷酷無情）：形容人的行為或性格特徵，缺乏同情心或感情。

The cold-hearted response to the charity appeal shocked everyone. 對慈善呼籲的冷酷回應讓每個人都感到震驚。

5. Indifferent（漠不關心）表示對某事物或情況缺乏興趣或關心，可能導致冷漠的行為。

He was indifferent to the suffering of others around him. 他對身邊人的痛苦漠不關心。

請注意，這些詞語都有著類似的含義，都指涉及冷漠、無情或缺乏情感的特質。

turn a blind eye to和turn a deaf ear to都表示「故意不理會」或「忽視某事或某人」的意思，但不一定都是負面的，也有正面特意忽略的意思。來看看例子：

1. The teacher decided to turn a blind eye to the student's minorrule violation this time. 老師這次決定對學生的小違規行為視而不見。

2. The manager chose to turn a blind eye to the employee's tardiness because he knew about their personal difficulties. 經理選擇對員工的遲到不予理睬，因為他知道他們的個人困難情況。

3. It's not wise to turn a blind eye to environmental problems; we should take action to address them. 對環境問題視而不見是不明智的；我們應該採取行動來解決它們。

Chinwag | 閒聊

Chinwag通常作名詞，指一次輕鬆、無目的性的閒聊、交談或聊天。有時也可以用作動詞，表示進行這樣的談話。

請參考以下應用的例句

1. We had a nice chinwag over a cup of tea yesterday. 昨天我們一邊喝茶一邊愉快地聊天。
2. After work, we often gather at the pub for a chinwag. 下班後，我們經常在酒吧聚在一起閒聊。
3. I called my old friend just to chinwag and catch up. 我打電話給我的老朋友，只是想聊聊天並聊聊近況。

Chinwag的同義字詞及例句

1. Chat輕鬆的對話或交談

   We had a pleasant chat over coffee this morning. 今早我們在喝咖啡時進行了一次愉快的聊天。

2. Conversation交談、談話

   Their conversation lasted for hours, covering various topics. 他們的談話持續了好幾個小時，涵蓋了各種主題。

3. Gossip有關他人私事的談話或八卦

   The office is buzzing with gossip about the new manager. 辦公室裡充滿了有關新經理的八卦。

4. Chitchat閒聊

We engaged in chitchat while waiting for the bus. 在等公車的時候，我們進行了閒聊。

Chinwag的同義詞通常指的是輕鬆、非正式的交談或聊天，可以在不同情境下使用，如朋友間的閒聊、社交場合中的交談，或是同事之間的輕鬆對話。

Clinch │ 緊緊抓住／成交

Clinch成交（動詞）

意指確定或決定某事，通常指達成一項協議、勝利或結束爭論。

1. After hours of negotiation, they finally clinched a deal. 經過幾小時的談判，他們最終達成了一項協議。
2. The team's victory was clinched with a last-minute goal. 這支球隊在最後一刻的進球確保了他們的勝利。
3. His outstanding performance clinched his promotion to manager. 他出色的表現確保了他升職為經理。

Clinch「緊緊抓住」（動詞）

也可以指緊緊握住或固定某物，為了防止其移動或鬆動。

1. He used nails to clinch the loose boards together. 他用釘子把鬆動的木板緊緊固定在一起。
2. The wrestler clinched his opponent to gain an advantage. 那位摔角手抓住對手以獲得優勢。
3. She clinched the lid tightly to keep the container airtight. 緊緊關上蓋子，以保持容器密封。

Clinch在這些情境中可以表示確定、緊緊握住或固定物的動作或意義。當表示「成交」時，clinch的同義詞可以是seal或conclude。當表示「緊緊抓住」時，同義詞可以是grasp或grip。

相關的英文應用

1. Seal（成交的同義詞）

   After weeks of negotiations, they finally sealed the deal. 經過數週的談判，他們終於達成了協議。

2. Conclude（成交的同義詞）

   The two parties concluded the agreement with a handshake. 兩方用握手來完成這項協議。

3. Grasp（緊緊抓住的同義詞）

   She grasped the rope tightly to avoid falling. 她緊緊抓住繩子以避免摔下來。

4. Grip（緊緊抓住的同義詞）

   He had to grip the steering wheel firmly to control the car. 他必須牢牢握住方向盤以控制車子。

Compose vs Manipulate
| 合成／竄改

名人頭像頻頻遭盜用，來看一下這段文字中這兩個單字在文章中要怎麼運用：

Celebrities are frequently subjected to their photos being composed and manipulated by scam groups or their social media profiles and videos being hijacked. People are concerned that if this behavior is not stopped promptly, the number of victims of these scams may continue to grow.

名人經常成為詐騙團體合成和竄改其照片，或劫持其社交媒體個人資料和影片的對象。大家擔心如果不立即阻止這種行為，被盜的詐騙人數可能會越來越多。

Compose（動詞）

指創作、構成或編寫某事物，通常指音樂、詩歌、文章或藝術創作。當需要表達創作或製作某些有組織或藝術性的東西時，可以用Compose。雖然Compose通常用來表示創作、組合或編排元素，但意思不限圖片的合成。它可以指將不同的元素組合成整體，這些元素可以是文字、圖片、音樂等。關於圖片的Compose，指將多張圖片合成一張，我們也常使用Merge或Combine。來瞭解一些英文例子：

1. She is known for her ability to compose beautiful and emotional music. 她以創作美麗且感人的音樂而聞名。

2. The artist took years to compose this intricate painting. 這位藝術家花了數年時間來創作這幅精細的畫作。

3. Can you compose a formal letter for me to send to the company? 你能幫我撰寫一封正式的信，我要寄給公司。

4. I need to compose a collage of photos for the art exhibition. 我需要為藝術展覽合成一個照片拼貼。

5. He composed a stunning image by merging several photographs together. 他通過合併幾張照片創作了一張令人驚嘆的圖像。

6. The graphic designer used Photoshop to compose the final product. 平面設計師使用Photoshop來合成最終成品。
所以Compose可以用來描述圖片的合成。

Manipulate（動詞）

指以欺騙、控制或改變方式處理或操作某事物，通常帶有負面的含義。當需要描述某人以不誠實或不正當的方式操縱、控制或影響某事物時，可以使用Manipulate。

1. The con artist tried to manipulate the stock market for personal gain. 詐騙犯試圖操縱股市以個人獲利。（註：Con artist是英語俚語，意思是「詐騙犯、騙子」。通常是在一段時間內以巧妙的方式欺騙受害者，可能涉及心理手段或狡猾的技巧。詐騙犯常精心策劃騙局，表現出迷惑和欺騙的專業技巧。）

2. It's important to be cautious of advertisements that aim to manipulate your emotions to make a sale. 對於旨在操縱你的情感以完成銷售的廣告要保持警惕是很重要的。

3. The evidence showed that the data had been manipulated to support a false conclusion. 證據顯示數據已被篡改以支持虛假的結論。

希望這些說明和例句能幫助您更好地理解Compose和Manipulate這兩個詞的用法和含義。

Compose同義詞

1. Create（創造）

She created a beautiful piece of artwork. 她創作了一幅美麗的藝術品。

2. Construct（建構）

They constructed a detailed plan for the project. 他們為該項目建構了詳細的計劃。

3. Assemble（組裝）

He assembled a team of experts to work on the project. 他召集了一個專家團隊來參與該項目。

Manipulate同義詞

1. Control（控制）

He tried to control the outcome of the experiment. 他試圖控制實驗的結果。

2. Handle（處理）

She knows how to handle difficult situations. 她知道如何處理困難的情況。

3. Influence（影響）

The media can influence public opinion. 媒體可以影響公眾意見。

請注意，這些同義詞在特定上下文中可能有些微不同的含義或用法，但它們通常可以用來代替Compose和Manipulate。

Composite | 複合材料

Composite可以是名詞、形容詞或動詞，至於這個單字的應用者要取決於當時的情境及上下文要如何使用：

Composite作為名詞
指由多個不同部分或成分組成的結構或整體。這可以是指材料、圖像、音樂或任何其他事物的組合。

1. This material is a composite of fiberglass and resin. 這個材料是由玻璃纖維和樹脂的複合物製成的。
2. This painting is a composite that incorporates different artistic styles from different periods. 這幅畫是一幅複合畫，包括了不同時期的藝術風格。

Composite作為形容詞
意指由不同元素或成分混合而成的，具有多樣性的特徵。

1. The car's body is made of composite materials, making it lightweight and strong. 這輛汽車的車身是由複合材料製成的，因此非常輕巧而堅固。
2. This is a composite image featuring mountains, lakes, and forests. 這是一幅複合圖像，包括了山脈、湖泊和森林。

Composite作為動詞
意指將不同元素或成分結合在一起，形成整體。

 FancyEnglish 精湛英文

1. We need to composite these data elements into a single comprehensive report. 我們需要將這些數據合成一份完整報告。

2. This song was composited by multiple singers working together. 這首歌曲是由多位歌手合唱共同創作的。

Composite的同義詞以及例子應用

1. Compound（複合化合物）：指由兩個或更多部分組成的整體。

   The chemical reaction produced a compound with unique properties. 化學反應產生了一種具有獨特性質的化合物。

2. Complex（複雜的）：指事物具有多個部分或層次，不容易理解或處理。

   Solving this complex mathematical problem requires advanced knowledge. 解決這個複雜的數學問題需要高級知識。

3. Composite（複合的）：根據前面的解釋，指由多個不同部分或成分組成的結構或整體。

   The composite materials used in the aircraft make it extremely durable. 飛機使用的複合材料使其極其耐用。

4. Mixture（混合物）：指不同成分或元素的組合，它們保持其獨立性。

   The salad is a delicious mixture of vegetables and herbs. 這個沙拉是蔬菜和香草的美味混合物。

Culpable
| 有責任不一定有罪唷

Culpable是形容詞，意思是「有罪的」或「應受責備的」，用來形容一個人或事物負有法律或道德的責任或過失。

一起來看應用在文章中的情形：

In our country's constitutional court, it is emphasized that such witness statements, not subject to on-the-spot cross-examination or questioning of the accused, may not be used as the exclusive or principal evidence for a court to find the accused culpable. This is done to strike a balance between discovering the truth for significant public interest and safeguarding the accused right to a fair in the court.

我們國家的憲法法院，強調證人陳述，未進行交叉詢問或質疑，不得作爲法院認定被告有罪的唯一或主要證據。這是爲了在追求重大公共利益的眞相發現與保障被告在法庭上享有公平審判權之間取得平衡而採取的措施。

Culpable的例句及應用

1. He was found culpable of stealing company funds, and now he's facing legal consequences. 他被判定有罪竊取公司資金，現在正面臨法律後果。

2. The evidence presented in court made it clear that the

defendant was culpable for the accident. 在法庭上呈現的證據清楚顯示被告對這次事故負有責任。

3. Culpable negligence can lead to serious harm to others, and it's important to act responsibly. 有罪的疏忽可能對他人造成嚴重傷害，負責任行事非常重要。

Culpable的同義詞及片語

1. Guilty（有罪的）

   She was found guilty of the crime and sentenced to prison. 她被判有罪並被判入獄。

3. Responsible（負責任的）

   The manager is responsible for the team's performance. 經理對團隊的表現負有責任。

4. At fault（有過失的）

   The driver who ran the red light was at fault in the accident. 闖紅燈的司機在事故中有過失。

5. Accountable（應負責任的）

   As the CEO, he is accountable for the company's success or failure. 作爲CEO，他應對公司的成功或失敗負責。

Reproachable、Censurable、Reprovable和Blameworthy都有責難或指責的意思，在某種程度上與Culpable相關，但有細微的不同。

1. Reproachable（可責難的）：指的是行爲或事情可能受到責難或譴責，但不一定意味著具體的法律責任。強調了

道德或社會上的不應該行爲。

Her careless behavior at the party was reproachable, and it embarrassed her friends. 她在派對上的粗心行爲令人責難，並讓她的朋友感到尷尬。

2. Censurable（應受譴責的）：更強調行爲受到公開譴責或批評，可能是違反了法律或社會規範，因此可能帶有法律責任。

The company's unethical practices are censurable and have led to public outrage. 該公司的不道德做法應受譴責，並引起了公憤。

3. Reprovable（可指責的）：也指的是行爲或事情可被指責或譴責，通常是出於道德或倫理原因。

His reprovable conduct during the meeting disrupted the entire discussion. 他在會議期間的可指責行爲破壞了整個討論。

4. Blameworthy（應受責備的）：His blameworthy actions led to the project's failure. 他應受責備的行爲導致了該項目的失敗。

Culpable更強調法律上的責任，指涉及罪行或過失，可能會面臨法律追究。因此有一些相似之處，但它們的使用上有些微的差異。

Cupidity｜貪婪

Cupidity是名詞，它的形容詞為Cupidious，貪婪的、貪心的。

一則有關泰國政府嚴懲貪心計程車司機的報導，來看一下如何用這字彙到文章之中：

Greed led to trouble as reported by Thai media. A Taiwanese female tourist arrived at a Thai airport and took a taxi to Bangkok, only to be charged 1200 to 1500 Thai Baht（approximately 1150 to 1440 New Taiwan Dollars） by a cupidious driver using a fabricated price list, which was over four times the regular fare. The Thai government has stated that they will severely penalize this taxi driver, banning them for life from picking up passengers at the largest Thai airport and possibly revoking their taxi license.

貪心導致麻煩，根據泰國媒體的報導。一名台灣女性觀光客抵達泰國機場後，搭計程車前往曼谷市區，卻被一位貪婪的司機以一份偽造的價目表收1200至1500泰銖的費用（約相當於1150至1440新台幣），這個價格遠高於準的計程車計費表，超過了標準費用的四倍以上。泰國政府已宣布將對這名程車司機實施嚴厲的懲罰，包括終身禁止在泰國最大的機場載客，並有可能銷他們的計程車執照。

來看看幾個例子

1. The cupidity of public figures has led to public scrutiny and the shattering of their own image of integrity, truly a loss that cannot be compensated. 公眾人物的貪婪行徑造成了民眾的質疑及自己清廉形象的破滅，真是得不償失。

2. Corruption is often fueled by the cupidity of politicians seeking personal gain over the welfare of their constituents. 腐敗常因為政治人物的貪婪驅使，他們追求個人利益而不是選民的福祉。

Dawdle | 打混

Dawdle動詞，有磨蹭、打混、遊手好閒及懶散的意思，以下為各種情境的例句說明：

The newcomers have been dawdling and arriving at work almost 2 hours late, which earned them a stern reprimand from HR: This does not work at all. 新進人員一直在遊手好閒，到工作場所幾乎晚了將近2小時，這使他們受到人力資源部的嚴厲譴責：這一點都不行。

1. 拖延，浪費時間

   Don't dawdle, we need to finish this project by tomorrow. 不要拖延，我們明天必須完成這個項目。

2. 閒逛，徘徊

   We spent the afternoon dawdling around the city, exploring its hidden corners. 我們整個下午都在城市裡閒逛，探索它的隱藏角落。

3. 懶散，慢吞吞

   She dawdled through her chores, taking twice as long as usual. 她做家務懶散，用的時間是平時的兩倍。

4. 磨蹭

   Stop dawdling and get ready for school! 別再磨蹭了，準備去上學吧！

Dawdle的同義詞

1. Linger（逗留）

   She likes to linger in the park after work. 她喜歡下班後在公園逗留。

2. Loiter（閒晃）

   Teenagers often loiter around the mall on weekends. 青少年常常在週末在購物中心閒晃。

3. Procrastinate（拖延）

   Don't procrastinate; start your homework now. 別拖延，現在就開始做你的家庭作業。

4. Tarry（徘徊）

   He tarried at the doorway, unsure whether to enter or not. 他在門口徘徊，不確定要不要進去。

Debunk｜揭穿／揭發

Look for inconsistencies in their words and actions指查看一個人的言行是否一致，揭穿一個人的真面目之類。

一起來看新聞報導一位婦人被「假兒子」詐騙，結果被行員、警察揭穿的短文。學習如何將Debunk套用在短文之中：

An early morning news report reveals a situation where a woman received a call from her son, who claimed that her mobile phone number had been changed and she needed to re-add him on Line. Trusting his instructions, the woman complied. Shortly thereafter, the son contacted her via Line, explaining he was facing financial difficulties and urgently required her assistance in transferring 390,000 yuan. Without suspicion, the woman visited the bank to facilitate the in-person transfer. Fortunately, attentive bank staff detected something amiss, and following an investigation by on-site police officers, they advised the woman to dial her son using the old number to debunk the deceitful act, thus exposing the scamming group posing as her son.

一則早間新聞報導揭示了一種情況，一名婦人接到她的「兒子」來電，聲稱她的手機號碼已更改，需要重新在Line上加他為好友。相信對方的指示，婦人照做了。不久後，這位「兒子」通過Line聯繫她，解釋自己面臨財務困難，迫切需

要她協助匯款39萬元。婦人毫無懷疑地前往銀行辦理當面轉帳。幸運的是，細心的銀行工作人員察覺到了異常情況，並在現場警察的調查後，建議婦人撥打她的「兒子」的「舊號碼」以揭穿詐騙集團的欺騙行為，從而揭露了冒充她的「兒子」的詐騙集團。

關於「揭穿」一個人的假面具可以這麼說

Unmasking someone's facade

Exposing someone's facade

Debunking someone's facade

Debunk不只有針對「人」的揭發，也可以針對「事」

1. The investigation worked to debunk the conspiracy theories surrounding the event. 就是說明調查針對揭發事件的陰謀論。

2. The article aimed to debunk the misconceptions about climate change. 文章揭發有關於對於氣候變遷的一些誤解。

Declining birthrate and aging population
少子化、高齡化及泡沫化

少子化和高齡化的英文怎麼說？通常是以這樣來表示A declining birthrate and an aging population或是decreasing birthrate and an aging population。泡沫化直接以bubble以名詞或動詞形式來使用。

應用少子化和人口老化的短文：

In modern society, there are social issues and crises related to a declining birthrate and an aging population, and experts suggest that these problems are correspondingly associated with a real estate bubble. In other words, demographic changes like a decreasing birthrate and an aging population may have a negative impact on the real estate market, possibly reducing demand or causing price instability. Experts may believe that there is some connection or interaction between these two factors.

這句話的意思是，「在現代社會中，有與人口出生率下降和人口老齡化相關的社會問題和危機，專家指出這些問題相對應地與不動產泡沫有關。」換句話說，人口結構的變化，如出生率下降和人口老齡化，可能對不動產市場產生負面影響，可能會減少需求或導致價格不穩定。專家可能認為這兩者之間存在一定的聯繫或互動。

Declining birthrates and an aging population are two major trends in today's society. Declining birthrates refer to a decrease in the proportion of young people in the population, which may lead to a future shortage of the workforce. Conversely, population aging means that the proportion of elderly people is increasing, leading to pressures on healthcare and social welfare systems. The combination of these two trends could have profound economic and social impacts, necessitating the formulation of policies and strategies to address them and ensure the sustainable development of society.

少子化及人口老年化是當今社會的兩大主要趨勢。少子化指的是人口中年輕人口比例下降，這可能導致未來的勞動力不足。與之相對的是，人口老年化意味著老年人口比例上升，這將帶來醫療保健和社會福利壓力。這兩個趨勢的結合可能對經濟和社會產生深遠影響，需要制定政策和策略來應對，以確保社會的可持續發展。

Default｜債務違約

Defaulting on its debt repayments意思是「債務違約」未能按時償還債務。其他與Defaulting含有相似意思的英文表達方式包括：Failing to meet obligations、Noncompliance、Violation、Breach。這些都可以用來描述未能遵守協議或合約的情況。

可以應用於下面的例子

1. Evergrande has been working to renegotiate its agreements with creditors after defaulting on its debt repayments. 恆大（Evergrande）在債務違約後一直與債權人重新協商協議。

2 The government had to step in to help stabilize the economy when a major corporation went into default on its bonds. 當大型企業債券違約時，政府不得不介入幫助穩定經濟。

3. The real estate developer struggled to recover after a series of financial setbacks led to multiple instances of default. 在一連串的財務挫折導致違約後，房地產開發商努力復原。

Defeasance vs Desuetude vs Abolishment
│解除vs失效vs廢止

Defeasance英文解說是The action or process of rendering something null and void.。Defeasance是法律和金融術語，指通過支付債務的方式來解除或免除責任的行為。The disbandment of a South Korean idol group due to a member's military enlistment has caused egregious defeasance, leaving fans shocked and concerned. 因一名成員入伍，南韓知名男子天團被迫解散，引發了令人震驚和關切的defeasance（合約解除）事件。

Defeasance其它例句

1. The mortgage was discharged through a defeasance agreement after the borrower paid off the remaining balance. 借款人支付了剩餘的款項後，通過一份解除合約的協議來解除了抵押貸款。

2. The company used a defeasance strategy to retire its outstanding bonds ahead of schedule. 該公司使用了一種解除協議策略提前償還了未到期的債券。

3. The defeasance provision in the contract allowed the parties to nullify their obligations under certain conditions. 合約中的解除條款允許各方在特定條件下撤銷其義務。

Defeasance相似的單字，以及說明、例句

1. Termination（終止）：表示結束或終止協議、合約或關係。

   The termination of the partnership was a mutual decision. 合夥關係的終止是雙方共同決定的。

2. Cancellation（取消）：指的是取消或撤銷一項計劃、預約或合約。

   The cancellation of the flight was due to bad weather. 航班的取消是因爲惡劣的天氣。

3. Abrogation（廢除）：意味正式廢除或撤回法律、規定或協議。

   The abrogation of the old policy led to the adoption of a new one. 對舊政策的廢除導致了新政策的採納。

4. Annulment（廢除）：將合約、婚姻或協議視爲無效或無效。

   The annulment of their marriage was a relief for both parties. 他們婚姻的無效是雙方的解脫。

這些詞語都表示結束或取消協議或合約的行爲，但它們可能在特定情境中有些微差異。

Desuetude（廢止）與defeasance（解除合約）意義不同

· Defeasance指的是正式地解除或終止合約、協議或法律規定的行爲，通常是基於特定條件或事件的發生。

· Desuetude則指的是法律、習慣或規則因長期不使用或不

執行而變得不再有效或失去法律效力的情況。這是較爲特定的法律術語，通常用來描述法律規定或習慣因不活躍而被視爲已廢除。

關於**Desuetude**的英文例句

1. The old law fell into desuetude after decades of disuse, rendering it effectively obsolete. 這項老法律在數十年不使用後陷入了廢棄，使其事實上變得過時了。

2. The custom of sending handwritten letters has gradually faded into desuetude in the age of email and instant messaging. 在電子郵件和即時通訊的時代，手寫信的習慣逐漸淡出而變得不再常見。

3. Some archaic words in the language have fallen into desuetude and are no longer used in modern conversation. 語言中的一些古語詞已經逐漸廢棄，不再在現代對話中使用。

其他**desuetude**的同義詞以及英文例句

1. Obsolescence（過時）

   The rapid advancement of technology often leads to the obsolescence of older devices. 技術的快速進步通常導致舊設備的過時。

2. Disuse（不使用）

   The disuse of the old factory resulted in its gradual deterioration. 對這家老工廠的閒置導致了其逐漸惡化。

3. Inactivity（不活躍）

   The inactivity of the law enforcement agency raised concerns

 FancyEnglish 精湛英文

about public safety. 執法機構的消極引起了對公共安全的擔
憂。

因此，defeasance與desuetude不是同義詞，它們有不同的法
律和行為涵義。

Abolishment和Desuetude

- Abolishment指的是正式地取消或廢除某個法律、制度、規
  定、機構等，通常是經過明確的決策或法律程序。它強調
  了明確的行動或決策，將某事物移除或廢除。
- Desuetude則指的是某事物或規則因長期不使用、不執行
  或不遵守而變得無效或失去實際效力。它通常強調的是逐
  漸淡出或被遺棄的狀態，而不一定需要明確的行動或決
  策。

兩個詞彙都表示某事物的結束或失效，但abolishment更著重
於「主動的終止行為」，而desuetude更側重於事物「逐漸失
效」或「淡出的狀態」。

Defile｜玷污／褻瀆／污染

Defile通常作動詞，意思是玷污、污染。defile有時可以表示污辱或褻瀆，尤其是當它用於描述對某人或某事的不敬或侮辱行為時。可以指涉到對聖地、價值觀念、人格或名譽的不敬行為。的中文同義詞可能包括：

Defile作「玷污」解釋時的同義字

1. Contaminate（污染）
2. Pollute（汙染）
3. Taint（玷污）
4. Desecrate（褻瀆）
5. Infect（感染）
6. Spoil（損壞）
7. Dirty（弄髒）
8. Corrupt（腐敗）

Defile表示「污辱」或「褻瀆」時的同義字

1. Profane（褻瀆）
2. Desecrate（褻瀆）
3. Insult（汙辱）
4. Disrespect（不敬）
5. Offend（冒犯）
6. Blaspheme（通常用於對宗教事物的不敬）
7. Degrade（貶抑）

這些詞語都可以用來描述某物或某地受到損害、污染或玷污的情況，具體的詞語選擇可能會根據上下文而有所不同。

Defile應用的例句及翻譯

The factory's waste disposal practices defile the nearby river, causing harm to the environment and wildlife. 這家工廠的廢棄物處理方式玷污了附近的河流，對環境和野生動植物造成了傷害。

Defile的同義字

當這些單字用於表示污辱、褻瀆或不敬時，它們的意思如下：

1. Taint（玷污）：指某物被污染或受到損害，特別是在道德或精神上。

   The scandal tainted the reputation of the company. 醜聞玷污了公司的聲譽。

2. Desecrate（褻瀆）：表示對聖地、神聖物品或價值觀念的不敬或褻瀆。

   Vandals desecrated the church by spray-painting graffiti on its walls. 破壞者在教堂的牆上塗鴉，褻瀆了這座教堂。

3. Blaspheme（褻瀆）、blasphemy（褻瀆的話語或行為）：通常用於對宗教事物或神的不敬，包括冒犯宗教教義或使用不適當的言語。

   He was accused of blasphemy for his comments about the sacred texts. 他因對聖典的評論而被指控犯了褻瀆罪。

4. Profane（褻瀆）：表示對宗教、聖地、神聖物品或價值

觀念的不敬或褻瀆。也可以用來描述粗俗或不適當的語言或行為。

Using the Lord's name in vain is considered a profane act by many believers. 在無數信徒看來，妄稱上帝的名字是一種褻瀆的行為。

Deludge｜洪水

除了Flood外，Deluge也是。deluge意指大量湧入的液體，常用來形容暴雨、洪水等極端降水情況（Inclement climate）。
The worst deluge in living memory. 這是有生以來最嚴重的洪水。這個字還有「大量湧登入」的意思，像是大量湧入的電話或需求。
洪水的同義詞：flood、inundation、torrent、downpour；反義詞乾旱：drought、scarcity

以下是幾個**Deluge**的應用方式

1. After the heavy rain, a deluge of water rushed down the streets, flooding homes and businesses. 大雨過後，洪水沖垮街道，淹沒了房屋和商店。

2. The sudden deluge of requests overwhelmed the server's capacity, causing it to crash. 突如其來的海量請求壓垮了服務的量能，導致崩潰。

3. The region experienced a deluge of snow during the winter months, leading to travel disruptions. 地區的冬季大雪，導致交通中斷。

4. The company was hit by a deluge of complaints from dissatisfied customers after the product recall. 產品的召回後，公司受到大量不滿意顧客的投訴。

Descant vs Annotate vs Expound

這三個單字的都是動詞，意思有些相關，但仍有差異。

1. Descant（動詞）以評論、論述或探討的方式討論某個主題。

   Political parties have the responsibility to descant on their stance regarding national positioning, core values, and governing theories, ensuring that the public fully comprehends their vision. 政黨有責任對國家定位、核心價值和治國理論進行詳細解釋，確保公眾充分理解他們的願景。

   She would often descant upon the virtues of a healthy lifestyle. 她經常對健康生活方式的優點進行評論。

2. Annotate（動詞）在書、文章或文件中加入註釋或評論，以解釋或標記重要訊息。

   Students were asked to annotate the text to highlight key concepts. 學生被要求對文本進行註釋，以突顯關鍵概念。

   The historian spent hours annotating historical documents for research purposes. 歷史學家花了幾個小時為研究目的對歷史文獻進行註釋。

3. Expound（動詞）詳細解釋或闡述某個主題、觀點或理論。

   The professor proceeded to expound upon the intricacies of quantum physics. 教授繼續闡述量子物理學的細節。

   In his lecture, the philosopher will expound his theories on ethics and morality. 哲學家在他的講座中將闡述他的倫理和道德理論。

這三個詞都涉及解釋或論述，但用法和重點略有不同。
Descant主要是關於討論或論述主題，通常不涉及註釋。
Annotate專注於在文本中添加註釋或評論以提供解釋。
Expound則是更廣泛的詳細解釋或闡述某個主題或觀點。

Destitute │ 赤貧的

Destitute是形容詞，形容某人非常貧困或一無所有的情況。

According to the Asian Development Bank（ADB）, as of last year, the COVID-19 pandemic and the rising cost of living have led to an increase of nearly 70 million destitute people in developing countries across Asia, undermining the efforts of these nations in combating poverty.

亞洲開發銀行（ADB）表示，截至去年，新冠疫情和生活成本上升，已導致亞洲開發中國家的極端貧困人口多了近7000萬人，破壞各國在打擊貧窮上付出的努力。

Destitute的英文例句及應用

1. She grew up in a destitute neighborhood, where basic necessities were often hard to come by. 她在一個貧困的社區長大，基本生活必需品常常難以獲得。

2. The earthquake left many families destitute, without homes or possessions. 地震使許多家庭變得赤貧，無家可歸，沒有財產。

和Destitute相近意思的單字與例句

1. Impoverished（赤貧的）

   Many families in the drought-stricken region were left

impoverished and struggling to feed themselves. 乾旱地區的許多家庭變得赤貧，勉強維持生計。

2. Penniless（一文不名的）

After losing his job, he was left penniless and had to rely on charity for food and shelter. 失業後，他變得一文不名，不得不依賴於慈善機構獲得食物和庇護。

3. Indigent（貧困的）

The indigent population in the city struggled to access basic healthcare services. 城市裡的貧困人口難以獲得基本的醫療服務。

4. Needy（貧困的）

The charity organization provides assistance to the needy, including food and clothing. 這家慈善組織為貧困人士提供援助，包括食物和衣物。

Dexterity | 靈巧

Dexterity靈巧、敏捷，指身體或手部的靈活和敏捷能力。在各種工藝、技術、運動、音樂和藝術領域，強調執行複雜或細緻任務時的技能和靈活性。其意思類似skill in（例：His skill in coding and problem-solving landed him a high-paying job at a prestigious tech company.）、be good at、be proficient in（例：She became proficient in playing the piano after years of dedicated practice.）可應用於醫術、音樂大師的專精和裁縫師的技藝。

請看以下Dexterity 的例子及應用

1. The surgeon's dexterity allowed for precise and intricate movements during the surgery. 醫生的靈巧程度使得手術過程中的動作精準而複雜。

2. The pianist's dexterity on the keys amazed the audience as he played complex compositions flawlessly. 鋼琴家的琴鍵靈巧程度讓觀眾驚嘆不已，他完美地演奏了複雜的樂曲。

3. The tailor's dexterity in sewing intricate patterns resulted in beautifully designed garments. 裁縫師熟練地縫製複雜的圖案，製作出設計精美的服裝。

Diabetes｜糖尿病

必須知道的一些糖尿病相關「醫學英文詞彙」

1. 糖尿病（Diabetes）
2. 盛行率（Prevalence Rate）
3. 空腹血糖（Fasting Blood Sugar）
4. 糖化血色素（Glycated Hemoglobin）
5. 後遺症（Complications）
6. 心血管疾病（Cardiovascular diseases）
7. 心肌梗塞（Myocardial Infarction or Heart Attack）
8. 神經病變（Neuropathy）
9. 視網膜病變（Retinopathy）
10. 腎臟病（Kidney Disease）
11. 糖尿病足病（diabetic foot problems）
12. 潰瘍（ulcerations）

The latest findings from the National Health Research Institutes reveal that the standardized prevalence rate of undiagnosed diabetes is approximately around 1%, estimating that about 220,000 people are unaware that they have diabetes.

國家衛生研究院的最新研究發現，未經診斷的糖尿病標準患病率約爲1%，估計約有22萬人不知道他們患有糖尿病。

According to the World Health Organization's definition of abnormal fasting blood sugar levels, it falls within the range of 110 to 125 mg/dL. According to the Diabetes Education Society, the normal range for glycated hemoglobin（HbA1C） is generally between 4.0% and 5.6%. Values between 5.7% and 6.4% are considered elevated, indicating a risk of developing diabetes, while values higher than 6.5% confirm a diagnosis of diabetes.

根據世界衛生組織對於異常的空腹血糖水平的定義，正常範圍在110到125毫克/分升之間。根據糖尿病教育學會的定義，糖化血紅蛋白（HbA1C）的正常範圍通常在4.0%至5.6%之間。5.7%至6.4%之間的數值被認為是升高的，表示有患糖尿病的風險，而高於6.5%的數值確診為糖尿病。

When diabetes becomes severe, it can lead to various complications, such as cardiovascular diseases, often causing conditions like heart disease and stroke; kidney disease that damages kidney function; neuropathy, retinopathy, diabetic foot problems, and ulcerations.

糖尿病嚴重時可是會引發多種後遺症，像是心血管疾病，常造成包括心臟病和中風；腎臟病變損害腎臟功能；神經病變、視網膜病變及糖尿病足病和傷口潰瘍等。

So, everyone must diligently control blood sugar, maintain target glucose levels, choose a low-sugar, low-fat, high-fiber diet, control calorie intake, engage in regular exercise to enhance heart health and reduce the risk of obesity. Additionally, control blood pressure and cholesterol to lower the risk of cardiovascular problems, and regularly monitor and check for diabetes.

所以啦，大家一定要好好控制血糖，保持血糖標準，飲食選擇低糖、低脂肪、高纖維的飲食，控制卡路里攝入，規律運動增強心臟健康，減少肥胖風險；並且控制血壓和膽固醇，保持健康的血壓和膽固醇降低心血管風險，定期監控及檢查糖尿病。

Diffident | 心虛

Diffident是形容詞，缺乏自信的、心虛膽小的。

同義字包括：shy、timid、reserved、insecure、bashful等。

She felt diffident about her testimony. 她對於自己的證詞感到心虛。

The man, diffident after driving under the influence, fled the scene, crashing his vehicle into a utility pole, and now faces charges of public endangerment. 這名男子，在酒後駕車後感到心虛，逃離現場，撞斷了電桿，現在面臨公共危險罪的指控。

將Diffident應用在句子中

1. The young lawyer's diffident attitude before bars contrasted with his usual confident demeanor. 年輕律師在法庭前缺乏自信的態度與他日常自信的表現形成了對比。

2. The defendant's testimony in the courtroom was quite diffident, lacking confidence and clarity in his statements. 法庭內被告提供證詞時，表現顯得相當心虛，缺乏自信而且言辭含糊。

3. His diffident nature made it difficult for him to make friends easily. 他的內向的性格使他很難輕易交到朋友。

Digress | 離題

Digress是動詞，偏離主題、離題。在談話或寫作中，當某人不再集中於原本的主題而開始講述或討論與主題無關的事情時，就可以使用。

Digress可以這樣使用，應用到下面這段文章之中：

In the 2023 College Entrance Exam（學測）for English, the essay prompt revolved around the topic of emoji and the potential misunderstandings and difficulties they may cause. According to the examiners, it was crucial for candidates to address the aspect of causing misunderstandings or difficulties. Those who lacked experiences related to this aspect might digress from the topic, risking point deductions if they focused solely on positive experiences.

在2023年的學測英文科作文題目圍繞著「表情符號（emoji）」的主題，以及它們可能引起的誤解和困擾。主考官表示，考生有必要討論「引起誤解或困擾」的方面。那些缺乏與此相關經驗的人可能會偏離主題，如果他們僅關注正面經驗，則可能會被扣分。（註：Essay prompts作文題目、文章題目。）

Here, the term digress is used to emphasize the importance of staying on-topic and not straying into unrelated areas when responding to the essay prompt. 在這裡digress一詞用來強調回答作文題目時保持不偏離主題。

Digress的幾個例句

1. He tends to digress during meetings, often going off on unrelated tangents, which can be quite distracting. 他在會議中往往會離題，經常講一些與主題無關的事情，這可能會分散注意力。

2. Please stick to the topic and avoid digressing into unrelated issues. 請集中於主題，避免陷入無關的議題。

3. While giving a presentation, she began to digress into personal anecdotes, which made the audience lose interest. 在做報告時，她開始講述個人趣聞軼事，這讓觀眾失去了興趣。

Digress的同義詞和應用例句

1. Deviate（偏離）：指偏離原有的路線、主題或計劃。

   During the hike, we deviated from the trail and got lost in the woods. 在徒步旅行中，我們偏離了小徑，迷失在樹林中。

2. Diverge（分歧、分開）：表示觀點、路線或事情分開或分歧。

   Their opinions began to diverge as they discussed the controversial issue. 當他們討論這個爭議性問題時，他們的意見開始分歧。

3. Ramble（閒聊、漫談）：指在講話或寫作中無計劃地漫談，常常跳來跳去。

   She tends to ramble when telling stories, making it hard to follow her narrative. 她講故事時經常閒聊，讓人難以理解她的敍述。

4. Wander（漫遊、流連）：表示在說話或行動中走離原路，通常指無目的地遊蕩或思緒飄忽。

He wandered off-topic during the discussion, talking about unrelated matters. 他在討論中離題，談論與主題無關的事情。

5. Stray（偏離、迷路）：表示偏離原路、主題或方向，有時指意外地迷路。

Try not to stray too far from the main idea when presenting your argument. 在提出你的論點時，盡量不要偏離主要思路。

Divest｜撤資

Divest動詞，撤資、出售、轉讓或放棄權益、財產或投資之意。通常用於商業、金融和社會議題上，表示結束與某項資產或事務的關聯，是出於道德、財務或策略性的考慮。

來閱讀一篇關於中國經濟成長放緩及其他不利綜合因素，造成外資及企業紛紛撤資的現象學，一起來瞭解Divest在文章中應用的情境及扮演的角色：

Concerns over China's economic outlook are driven by a combination of factors. The deceleration of the Chinese economy and unsatisfactory data are primary concerns. Additionally, the instability stemming from legal changes, the depreciation of the Renminbi, and insolvencies in the real estate sector have led to a wave of foreign divestment from Chinese stocks, accelerating capital withdrawals. Small and medium-sized enterprises also plan to divest or relocate investments, further exacerbating the vicious cycle of capital outflows.

對於中國經濟前景的擔憂等多種因素。中國經濟放緩和不滿意的數據是主要擔憂。此外，法律變動帶來不穩定性、人民幣貶值以及不動產業的破產，已導致外國加速撤資中國股票。小型和中型企業也計劃撤資或轉移投資，進一步加劇了資金外流的惡性循環。

Divest的英文實例應用

1. The company decided to divest its underperforming divisions to improve its overall profitability. 該公司決定出售表現不佳的部門，以提高整體盈利能力。

2. Many universities have divested from fossil fuel investments as part of their commitment to combating climate change. 許多大學已經退出了化石燃料投資，作爲他們對抗氣候變化的承諾的一部分。

3. The government announced its intention to divest its ownership stake in several state-owned enterprises to stimulate private sector growth. 政府宣布了將出售其在幾家國有企業中的股權的意圖，以刺激私營部門的增長。

Divest的使用情境包括企業策略、環境保護和投資組合管理等領域，它強調了放棄或轉移資產的行動，以達到特定的目標或價值觀。

Divest的同義詞、片語及例句

1. Disinvest撤資（動詞）

   The company decided to disinvest from its overseas operations due to financial difficulties. 由於財務困難，該公司決定從海外業務中撤資。

2. Sell off賣掉（動詞片語）

   The investor chose to sell off their shares in the struggling tech company. 投資者選擇賣掉他們在陷入困境的科技公司的股份。

3. Dispose of 處置（動詞片語）

The government plans to dispose of its non-essential assets to reduce debt. 政府計劃處置其非必要資產以減少債務。

4. Liquidate 清算（動詞）

The bankrupt company had to liquidate its assets to pay off creditors. 這家破產的公司必須清算其資產以償還債權人。

Don't fob me off.
不要藉口搪塞我／不要敷衍我

類似Fob off表達方式

1. Brush off：Don't brush me off with excuses. 不要用藉口把我擺脫掉。

2. Give the runaround：I don't appreciate it when people give me the runaround. 我不喜歡別人拖拖拉拉地應對我。

3. Palm off：They tried to palm off their responsibilities onto someone else. 他們試圖把責任推卸給別人。

4. Stall：Stop stalling and give me a straight answer. 不要再拖延了，給我明確的答案。

5. Equivocate：Instead of giving a clear answer, he chose to equivocate and confuse the issue. 與其給出明確的回答，他選擇含糊其詞，混淆問題。

6. Prevaricate：Don't prevaricate; I need a straightforward response. 不要拖延，我需要坦率的回應。

7. Beat around the bush：He's always beating around the bush when I ask him important questions. 每當我問他重要問題時，他總是拐彎抹角。

Disfranchise | 剝奪公民權

Disfranchise是動詞，意思是剝奪某人的選舉權或公民權。

疫情期間有一則剝奪確診者投票公民權的相關報導，我們看一下如何將這個單字Disfranchise應用在文章之中：

A civic organization condemns the government for disfranchising the people by not following legal procedures. They believe that confirmed cases should be enfranchised to vote separately from the general public rather than requiring them not to go out to vote.

公民團體譴責政府未按照法律程序剝奪人民選舉權，他們認為應賦予確診者與一般民眾分流投票權利而非要求確診者不得外出投票。

分享幾個例句

1. The government's decision to disfranchise certain minority groups was met with widespread criticism. 政府剝奪特定少數族裔群體的參選權受到了廣泛的批評。

2. In the past, women were often disfranchised and denied the right to vote in many countries. 在過去，許多國家經常剝奪婦女的選舉權，拒絕她們投票的權利。

3. Efforts have been made to enfranchise previously disfranchised communities and ensure equal access to voting rights. 已採

取措施，以賦予先前被剝奪權利的社區參選權，確保平等獲得選舉權利。（註：enfranchise賦予選舉權、賦予公民權利，用來描述將一個人或群體納入選舉過程，允許他們參與選舉、投票，或享有公民權利的行為。與disfranchise相對，enfranchise強調賦予權利，而不是剝奪權利。）

Disfranchise通常用於討論政治權利和公民權利的問題，特別是當這些權利被剝奪或限制時。

Disfranchise的同義詞

1. Disenfranchise（動詞）：剝奪某人的選舉權或公民權。
   The dictator's regime sought to disenfranchise the opposition, preventing them from participating in elections. 獨裁者的政權試圖剝奪反對派的選舉權，阻止他們參加選舉。
2. Deprive of the franchise（片語）：剝奪某人的選舉權或公民權。
   The corrupt officials were accused of depriving citizens of the franchise through voter suppression. 貪污的官員被指控通過壓制選民剝奪了他們的選舉權。

Enfranchise的同義詞

1. Empower（動詞）：授予權力、權利或機會。
   Education can empower individuals by providing them with knowledge and skills. 教育可以通過提供知識和技能來賦予個人權力。

2. Grant suffrage（片語）：賦予選舉權。

The new law granted suffrage to all citizens over the age of 18. 新法賦予所有年滿18歲的公民選舉權。

Downtrodden ｜ 受到壓迫

Downtrodden形容詞，描述那些受到壓迫、處於困境、被欺凌或處於不利境地的人或群體。常用來強調他們的困境或不公平待遇。

來看一下Downtrodden在〈文化壓迫〉文章中如何應用：

The Chinese authorities claim to implement bilingual education in Tibet, but a United Nations expert report reveals that the Chinese government is engaging in cultural oppression through a compulsory and large-scale boarding school system. This system is affecting one million Tibetan children, leading to the assimilation of their culture, religion, and language. The forced use of Mandarin in their compulsory education is causing these downtrodden Tibetan students to lose their ability to use their mother tongue and eroding their cultural and identity.

中國當局聲稱在西藏實行「雙語教學」，但聯合國專家報告揭示，中國政府透過強制性的大規模寄宿學校體制，正在對一百萬名藏族兒童進行文化、宗教和語言上的同化。強制使用普通話進行義務教育使這些被壓迫的藏族學童「失去使用母語的能力」，並侵蝕了他們的文化和身分。（註：Assimilation同化，指一個文化或群體被迫或自願地融入另一個文化，使其失去獨特的特徵或身分。）

來看看例句應用

1. The downtrodden workers finally stood up for their rights and demanded better working conditions. 受壓迫的工人最終站起來爭取他們的權益，要求更好的工作條件。

2. The organization's mission is to provide assistance to the downtrodden and marginalized communities in the region. 這個組織的使命是為該地區受壓迫和被邊緣化的社區提供幫助。

3. In the novel, the protagonist is a symbol of hope for the downtrodden, inspiring them to believe in a better future. 這部小說中，男主角是受壓迫者希望的象徵，鼓舞他們相信有一個更美好的未來。

Downtrodden的同義詞

1. Oppressed（受壓迫的）：用來形容人們因種種原因而受到嚴重的不公平對待。

   The oppressed citizens of the country longed for freedom and equality. 這個國家受壓迫的公民渴望自由和平等。

2. Marginalized（被邊緣化的）：用來描述那些被社會邊緣化或排斥的人群。

   The marginalized communities in the city struggle to access basic resources and opportunities. 這個城市的被邊緣化社區努力獲得基本資源和機會。

3. Disadvantaged（處於不利地位的）：指的是那些因社會、經濟或其他因素而處於不利地位的人。

   The organization focuses on providing support to

disadvantaged children to help them break the cycle of poverty. 這個組織致力於爲處於不利地位的兒童提供支援，幫助他們打破貧困循環。

4. Subjugated（被征服的）：表示人們被強制服從或控制，通常是由權威或壓迫者實施。

The subjugated population rebelled against their oppressive rulers in search of freedom. 被征服的人民反抗壓迫統治者，追求自由。

這些相關詞彙都用來描述不同程度的壓迫、不公平對待或困境。

Dross │ 廢渣

Dross名詞，渣滓、無價值的東西。用於描述低質量、無價值或不重要的事物。

例句及其應用

1. The dross of the internet, such as spam emails and clickbait articles, can be quite annoying. 互聯網上的垃圾，如垃圾郵件和釣魚網站真的煩人。

2. He managed to filter out the dross from the valuable information in the research papers. 他成功地從研究論文中過濾出無價值的訊息。

3. The company's focus is on innovation, and they have little tolerance for dross that doesn't contribute to their goals. 這家公司專注於創新，對公司目標無貢獻價值的東西幾乎沒有容忍空間。

Dross強調某物的低價值，可用於各種情境中，包括描述事物的品質、價值或重要性。

Dross的同義詞

1. Junk：指無價值或低質量的東西，通常是指物品。

   The attic was filled with junk that hadn't been used in years. 閣樓裡堆滿了多年未用的廢物。

2. Trash：廢棄物、垃圾，通常指可以扔掉的東西。

   Please take out the trash before it starts to smell. 請在垃圾開始發臭之前把它拿出去。

3. Rubbish：廢棄物、垃圾，也可以指言論或觀點的無價值性。

   He sorted through the rubbish to find something of value in the old storage unit. 他在舊儲藏室中仔細搜查垃圾，希望找到有價值的東西。

4. Clutter：指雜亂無章、無秩序的東西。

   Her desk was filled with clutter, making it hard to find anything. 她的桌子上堆滿了雜亂的東西，很難找到任何東西。

5. Debris：碎片、殘骸，通常指毀壞或分解後的殘骸。

   After the explosion, the street was covered in debris from the damaged buildings. 爆炸後，街道上散落著受損建築物的碎片。

Drudgery | 苦差事

Dudgery名詞，指單調、乏味、枯燥且重複性高的工作或任務，苦差事。通常在談論沉悶、不感興趣或繁瑣的工作時會使用。

如何應用Drudgery，來看一下印度一則關於清潔工贏得彩票仍不放棄苦差事的文章：

In India, a group of sanitation workers toils tirelessly in the drudgery of garbage collection. Despite their meager daily wages, they supplement their incomes by selling recyclables. Surprisingly, they decided to pool their resources to purchase a 250 rupee （approximately 96 New Taiwan Dollars） lottery ticket, and their dreams unexpectedly came true! They won a whopping 100 million rupees（around 38 million New Taiwan Dollars）. However, even after hitting the jackpot, these sanitation workers have chosen to continue their laborious jobs. They joke that because working together is how we collectively invest in striking rich, so they're in it for the long haul.

在印度，一群清潔工人不知疲倦地努力幹著「苦差事」，收集垃圾。儘管他們每日微薄的工資，他們透過出售可回收物品來增加收入。令人驚訝的是，他們決定集資購買一張價值250盧比（約相當於96新台幣）的彩票，而他們的夢想意外地成眞了！他們贏得了一筆驚人的1億盧比（約相當於

3800萬新台幣）。然而，即使中了頭獎，這些衛生工人仍選擇繼續辛苦工作，並開玩笑說：因為我們共同努力工作是集體致富的方式，所以我們會長期堅持下去。（註：Toil in 勞苦於⋯辛勤工作於⋯。在上述文中，toil in the drudgery of garbage collection可翻譯成「在努力地幹著垃圾收集的苦差事」。）

Drudgery的其他例句應用

1. I can't stand the drudgery of data entry; it's the same thing every day. 我無法忍受每天都做相同的數據輸入工作，太單調了。

2. After years of drudgery in the corporate world, he decided to pursue his passion for painting. 在公司世界裡多年的苦差事之後，他決定追求他對繪畫的熱情。

3. The constant drudgery of housecleaning can be exhausting, but it's necessary to maintain a clean and healthy home. 持續不斷的家務工作可能會令人筋疲力竭，但為了保持乾淨和健康的家，這是必要的。

Drudgery的同義字詞

1. Monotony（單調）：指工作或活動的重複性和乏味性，通常令人感到厭倦。

   Her job involved a lot of monotony, as she had to perform the same tasks every day. 的工作很單調，因為她每天都要執行相同的任務。

2. Tedium（乏味）：表示工作或活動冗長無聊，令人感到厭煩。

The tedium of data entry tasks made him lose interest in his job. 資料輸入工作的乏味性讓他對工作失去了興趣。

3. Tediousness（冗長）：指工作或活動的冗長性，可能因其長時間而變得疲憊。

The tediousness of the meeting dragged on for hours without any meaningful discussion. 會議的冗長持續了數小時，卻沒有任何有意義的討論。

4. Grind（苦差事）：表示重複性的、沉悶的工作，通常需要長時間和耐心。

Working on the assembly line felt like a never-ending grind. 在裝配線上工作感覺像是無休止的苦差事。

5. Chore（苦差事）：形容日常生活中的乏味或不感興趣的任務。

Cleaning the garage is always such a chore. 清理車庫總是如此的苦差事。

  FancyEnglish 精湛英文

Duplicity | 雙面人

Duplicitous形容詞，名詞是Duplicity。雙面的、奸詐的，一種「雙重性格」，形容人表面上顯示友好或眞誠，但在背後採取欺騙性或不誠實的行爲或態度。

要形容政治人物是「雙面人」可以說：

This politician is a duplicitous individual who presents a friendly image to the public but often engages in behind-the-scenes dealings. 這位政治人物在公衆面前呈現友好形象，但常常在幕後進行一些不誠實的交易。

閱讀有關「旣迷人又警示的」短文，學習如何在利用此字：

Duplicity is the art of weaving a web of contradictions within one's character. It's the ability to exude charm and sincerity while concealing darker motives beneath the surface. In the world of politics, it's a common tool employed to win trust, only to betray it when expedient. Duplicity can be a survival tactic, a way to navigate treacherous waters, or a mask worn to secure personal gain. However, it's a precarious path, as the consequences of duplicity can lead to exposure and isolation. In a world where authenticity is valued, the allure of duplicity remains both captivating and cautionary.

雙面人是一種在個性中編織矛盾的藝術。它是在表面展現魅力和誠懇的能力，同時在內心深處隱藏更黑暗的動機。在政

治世界中，它是常見的工具，用來贏得信任，只有在方便的時候才背叛它。雙面人可以是一種生存策略、應對危險的方式，或是為了獲取個人利益而戴上的面具。然而，這是一條危險的道路，因為雙面人的後果可能導致暴露和孤立。在一個重視真實性的世界中，雙面人的魅力既迷人又警示。

與Duplicitous相近的英文單字或表達方式

1. Deceptive：具有欺騙性的，常用來描述引人上當的行為。
2. Two-faced：形容人在不同情境下表現出截然不同的兩面。
3. Dishonest：不誠實的，用來指代不真實或欺詐性的行為。
4. Scheming：具有策劃性的，通常指涉到陰謀或詭計的行為。
5. Double-dealing：雙重交往，表示在兩個不同的情境中採取不同行為或立場。
6. Duplicity：名詞，表示雙面性或欺騙行為。
7. Guileful：指某人狡詐、狡猾，能巧妙地欺騙或操控他人，可能是出於個人利益。

Guileful有欺騙的意思，但仍與Duplicitous有區別

1. Duplicitous指的是某人或某事具有欺騙性、虛偽或不誠實的特點，可能是在言語或行為上表現出來的。強調了「雙重性」或「虛假的」性質。
2. Guileful指的是某人具有「狡詐和狡猾」的特質，他們通常能夠巧妙地欺騙或操控他人，可能是出於個人利益。

應用例句如下

1. Duplicitous: His behavior was completely unexpected to us; he has been so duplicitous. 他的行為對我們來說是完全出乎意料的，他一直都是如此虛偽／雙面人格的。

2. Guileful: The guileful businessman successfully achieved his goals through various means. 那名狡猾的商人成功地以各種手段達成了他的目標。

Ebullient｜願你有個
充滿活力和快樂的一天！

May you have an ebullient and happy day! 願你有個充滿活力和快樂的一天！

Ebullient在句子或文章裡可以這樣應用：
The presidential candidate visited temples across the country, seeking to connect with the divine, to protect Taiwan's prosperity and the well-being of its people, to bring about favorable conditions, and to end the pandemic soon. It was an ebullient expression of hope for a vibrant Year of the Rabbit.
總統候選人到全國廟宇參拜，祈求神威顯赫，庇佑台灣國泰民安、風調雨順、疫情早日結束，也期許兔年是充滿活力希望的一年。Vibrant、dynamic、enthusiastic也有相同的意思。

Ebullient例句及應用

1. The concert was a showcase of the band's ebullient performance, leaving the audience in high spirits. 音樂會展現了樂隊熱情洋溢的表演，讓觀眾們精神抖擻。

2. Your ebullient personality and infectious laughter brightened up the room. 你熱情洋溢的個性和富有渲染力的笑聲讓整個房間都充滿了活力。

Echo Chamber｜同溫層

Echo chamber（同溫層）指的是一個情境或社交環境中，人們與持有相似觀點或立場的人互動，導致他們的想法和信仰被不斷地重複和強化，而不容易受到不同觀點的挑戰。可能導致偏見和對多元觀點的關閉。

科學上的「同溫層」Stratosphere則是用來描述大氣中的一個區域，其中溫度隨著高度的增加而增加，而不同於低溫的對流層。

在日常對話中，也可能用同溫層來比喻社交或思想上的環境，但Echo chamber更明確地強調了訊息的循環和加強，而不僅僅是溫度的變化。當人們僅在他們社交媒體圈子內與相似觀點的人互動時，他們可能陷入Echo chamber。

來看一篇短文，進一步瞭解如何運用Echo chamber：

In the realm of politics, it is imperative that political figures or parties strive to garner the broadest public support rather than remaining ensconced in the echo chamber of self-assurance. The term echo chamber aptly describes a situation where individuals or groups surround themselves with like-minded individuals, reinforcing their own beliefs and shutting out dissenting voices. This approach may lead to a false sense of security, insulated from the diverse perspectives and feedback of the wider population.

政治領域中，政治人物或政黨必須尋求最多人民的支持，而不是固守在自我感覺良好的「同溫層」中。詞語「同溫層」生動地描述了一種情況，即個人或團體將自己圍繞在思想相近的人群中，強化自己的信仰，排斥異議聲音。可能導致一種虛假的安全感，遠離更廣泛人民的多元觀點和反饋。

On the contrary, political actors must actively seek to engage with a wide spectrum of constituents, attentively listening to their concerns, and crafting policies that serve the greater good. By doing so, they can build a more inclusive and robust foundation of support. Avoiding the echo chamber and embracing a more inclusive approach is essential for a thriving democracy, one that truly represents the varied voices within society and leads to equitable and enduring policies.

相反，政治人物必須積極與各種不同背景的選民互動，仔細聆聽他們的關切，制定符合整體利益的政策。這樣做可以建立更包容和穩固的支持基礎。避免陷入「同溫層」，擁抱更包容的方式對於繁榮的民主至關重要，這樣的民主才能真正代表社會中多樣的聲音，並促成公平而持久的政策。（註：1. Remain持續存在或保持某種狀態。Ensconced安頓或舒適地安置在某處。remain ensconced持續保持在一個舒適或安全的位置或狀態中。2. Aptly副詞，描述某事以適當或適切的方式發生。表示某事情發生或表達得很恰當或合適。3. A wide spectrum指廣泛的或多種多樣的事物。A wide spectrum of constituents意指多樣性的成分或成員，可以包括各種不同的事物或群體。）

同溫層Echo chamber 的例句與應用

1. Many people unknowingly create an echo chamber on social media by only following and engaging with those who share their same beliefs. 許多人在社交媒體上不自覺地建立了同溫層，只追蹤和互動那些持有相同信仰的人。

2. In an echo chamber, people's opinions are constantly reinforced, making it difficult for them to consider alternative viewpoints. 在同溫層中，人們的觀點不斷被強化，使他們難以考慮其他觀點。

3. Breaking out of the echo chamber requires actively seeking out diverse perspectives and engaging in open dialogue with people who hold different beliefs. 要擺脫同溫層，需要積極尋求多元的觀點，並與持有不同信仰的人進行開放的對話。

同溫層Echo chamber是描述人們在社交媒體與持有相似觀點或立場的人互動，從而導致他們的信仰和觀點被不斷重複和強化的現象。

還可以這樣說

1. 資訊過濾泡（Filter Bubble）：這個術語強調了人們在網絡上只暴露於他們已有觀點的訊息，而不容易接觸到多元觀點。

The algorithm personalized his news feed so much that he was trapped in a filter bubble, only seeing content that reinforced his existing beliefs. 演算法個性化了他的新聞訂閱，以至

於他被困在資訊過濾泡中，只看到強化他現有信仰的內容。

2. 情感圈子（Bubble of Affirmation）：這個術語強調了在某些社交圈子中，人們傾向於互相確認和強化彼此的觀點，而不容易接觸到不同意見的聲音。

She surrounded herself with a tight-knit bubble of affirmation, where everyone agreed with her opinions, and dissenting voices were not tolerated. 她圍繞自己建立了一個緊密的情感圈子，在這個圈子裡，每個人都同意她的觀點，不同意見的聲音是不容忍的。

這些術語都描述了在不同情境中，人們如何被限制在一個訊息或意見的泡泡中，而不容易接觸到多元觀點。這些現象可能對個人的觀點和信仰產生強烈影響。

Efface │ 抹去

Efface動詞，抹去、擦去、消去、使不明顯或不突出。同義詞：Erase、Remove、Obliterate、Wipe out、Expunge、Rub out等。

Efface用於句子中的例子

1. To efface Taiwan's notorious reputation as a pedestrian hell, government transportation authorities are currently drafting new traffic regulations. 為了讓台灣除去行人地獄的惡名，政府交通單位正著手草擬新的交通法規。

2. She used an eraser to efface the pencil marks on the paper. 她用橡皮擦去了紙上的鉛筆痕跡。

3. Time had effaced the memory of their argument, and they were friends again. 時間已經抹去了他們爭吵的記憶，他們再次成為朋友。

4. The rain had effaced the chalk drawings on the sidewalk. 雨水已經抹去了人行道上的粉筆畫。

5. His modesty made him efface himself in social situations. 他的謙虛使他在社交場合中讓自己不明顯。

6. The new regulations aim to efface the negative impact of pollution on the environment. 新的規定旨在消除污染對環境的負面影響。

Egregious │ 震驚

Egregious形容詞，極其嚴重的、過分的或是震驚的。用來描述嚴重或引人注目的不當行為或情況。

The fact that the beautiful NANA performed a full nude scene with no substitute is truly egregious and shocking. 美女NANA沒有替身全裸演出是極其嚴重、令人震驚的。

Egregious的例句與應用

1. The company's egregious negligence in safety regulations resulted in a major industrial accident. 公司在安全法規上的極端疏忽導致了一起重大的工業事故。

2. Her egregious behavior at the formal dinner, including talking with her mouth full, shocked the other guests. 她在正式晚宴上的極其失禮行為，包括大口吃飯，讓其他客人感到震驚。

3. The politician's egregious misuse of public funds led to widespread outrage among the citizens. 政治家對公共資金的極其濫用引起了市民的廣泛憤怒。

其他具有類似意思的單字

1. Flagrant（明目張膽的）形容某事極為明顯且無法忽視的。

His flagrant disregard for the law led to his arrest. 他對法律的明目張膽無視導致了他的被捕。

2. Blatant（公然的）表示某事非常明顯，幾乎可以被公然看見。

The company's blatant disregard for environmental regulations is causing pollution. 公司對環保法規的公然無視導致了污染問題。

3. Outrageous（令人憤怒的）形容某事極為不合理或無法容忍，引起強烈的憤怒。

The outrageous prices at the luxury boutique left shoppers in disbelief. 奢侈精品店的高價格讓購物者難以置信。

Startle和Flagrant、Blatant或Outrageous不完全相同

Startle表示突然「受到驚嚇或吃驚」，通常描述「意外或突然」的驚嚇情況，與震驚有別。語義更偏向情感上的反應，不是對某事的評價。因此，雖然Startle可以用來描述某些令人震驚的情況，但它不具備Egregious、Flagrant、Blatant或Outrageous那種強烈批評或不滿的含義。

Elide vs Elude

Elide（動詞），省略或刪去一個詞、短語或句子

通常是爲了簡化或避免重複。

1. In order to make the text more concise, the author decided to elide some unnecessary details from the description. 爲了使文本更加簡潔，作者決定刪去描述中的一些不必要的細節。

2. Please elide the redundant information in this report to make it more focused on the key findings. 請刪去這份報告中多餘的訊息，使其更加聚焦於主要發現。

3. The editor suggested that we elide the repetitive dialogue in the screenplay to improve the pacing of the movie. 編輯建議我們刪去劇本中重複的對話，以改善電影的節奏。

Elude（動詞）逃避或躲避

通常指避免被抓住、理解或解決。

1. Despite his best efforts, the elusive criminal managed to elude the police for months. 儘管他盡了最大努力，這位難以捉摸的罪犯成功逃避了警方數月之久。

2. The answer to that riddle continues to elude me; I just can't figure it out. 那個謎語的答案依然讓我摸不著頭腦，我就是解不開。

3. Success can sometimes elude us, but with perseverance and

determination, we can achieve our goals. 成功有時會讓我們感到困難，但通過毅力和決心，我們可以實現目標。

Elide的同義詞

1. Omit（省略）：刪去或忽略部分，以簡化或改善清晰度。

   The editor decided to omit the lengthy introduction to make the article more concise. 編輯決定刪去冗長的引言使文章更簡潔。

2. Exclude（排除）：將某事物排除在考慮之外。

   Please exclude irrelevant data from your research findings. 請排除與研究結果無關的數據。

3. Skip（略過）：跳過或忽略一部分，通常因為不重要或不必要。

4. Remove（移除）：將某物或某事從中刪除或去除。

Elude的同義詞

1. Evade（躲避）：避免或逃避某事物，通常是負面的情況。

   The clever criminal managed to evade capture by constantly changing his hideout. 這位聰明的罪犯成功地躲避了被捕，不斷變換藏身之處。

2. Avoid（避免）：有意避開或不參與某事，以避免可能的問題或困難。

   She tried to avoid discussing the topic to prevent an argument from breaking out. 她試圖避免討論這個話題，以防止爭吵

發生。

3. Escape（逃脫）：成功地避開或逃離危險、責任或掌握。

4. Dodge（閃避）：快速移動或避開某物，通常是為了躲避危險、避免被擊中、或規避不想參與的事情。

The agile athlete managed to dodge the defender and score a goal. 靈活的運動員成功地閃避了防守球員，進球得分。

Elusive｜難以捉摸

Elusive形容難以理解、把握、捉摸的事物（科學）或概念。也用來描述難以實現或達到的目標或願望，像是常溫超導體room-temperature superconductor。相同概念的單字還有：Evasive、Slippery、Hard to grasp、Intangible、Impalpable、Evanescent、Uncatchable。

Elusive 的英文例句與應用

1. The answer to the room-temperature superconductor remained elusive, scientists feel frustrated. 常溫超導體的答案依然難以捉摸，柯學家們仍感到沮喪。

2. The truth behind the conspiracy theory remained elusive, with no concrete evidence to support it. 陰謀論背後的真相依然難以捉摸，沒有具體的證據支持。

3. Despite studying for hours, the solution to the math problem remained elusive to the students. 儘管花了幾個小時學習，這道數學問題的解答對學生們來說依然難以捉摸。

Emotionally vulnerable
玻璃心

先來看以下是這幾個單字的中文意思和用法：

Vulnerable（易受傷害、有弱點的）

描述人或事物容易受到傷害、打擊的情形。

1. The child's feelings are vulnerable, so be gentle with your words. 孩子的情感很脆弱，所以要用溫和的話語。
2. In times of crisis, a nation's economy can become vulnerable. 危機時刻，一個國家的經濟可能變得脆弱。
3. Vulnerable populations, like the elderly, need extra care during a pandemic. 脆弱的人口，比如老年人，在大流行期間需要額外的關懷。

Fragile（易碎的、脆弱的）

描述物品或情感容易受到破壞或傷害的特性。

1. Handle the glassware with care; it's very fragile. 小心處理這些玻璃器皿，它們很脆弱。
2. Their relationship is fragile right now, so avoid confrontations. 他們的關係現在很脆弱，所以要避免衝突。
3. The fragile ecosystem of the coral reef is under threat from climate change. 珊瑚礁這個脆弱的生態系統正受到氣候變化的威脅。

 FancyEnglish 精湛英文

Sensitive（感性的、敏感的）

形容人容易感受情感、環境或刺激的特性。

1. She is a very sensitive person and cries easily. 她是一個非常敏感的人，容易哭。

2. The microphone is so sensitive; it can pick up even the faintest sounds. 這個麥克風非常敏感，可以捕捉到最微弱的聲音。 3. Discussing that topic with him is tricky because he's very sensitive about it. 和他討論那個話題很棘手，因為他對此非常敏感。

前面放上情感敏感的Emotional，就表示玻璃心

1. Emotionally Fragile: Easily breakable or sensitive when it comes to emotions. This term implies that someone is easily hurt or upset by emotional experiences.

   She's emotionally fragile, so we need to be careful with our words. 她感情脆弱，所以我們要小心言辭。

2. Emotionally Vulnerable: Prone to being hurt or affected by emotional situations or stress. This term suggests a susceptibility to emotional harm.

   After the breakup, he felt emotionally vulnerable and needed support from friends. 分手後，他感到情感上脆弱，需要朋友的支持。

3. Emotionally sensitive: Highly attuned to emotions, often noticing and reacting to even subtle emotional changes. This term doesn't necessarily imply fragility but rather an acute awareness of emotions.

Her emotionally sensitive nature makes her an excellent therapist. 她的情感敏感性使她成爲一位優秀的心理治療師。

這些詞彙都可以用來描述玻璃心，但有不同的意義和用法，具體取決於情境和強調的方面，這樣了解了嗎？

Emphatic │ 強調的

Emphatic強調的、著重的或明確的，表示對某事物或觀點的強調，強烈支持或否定。

例句

1. Presidential candidate during a recent interview emphatically stated that currently we have enough electricity, and there will be no issues with a stable power supply! 總統參選人在最近的一次訪問中強調表示，目前我們擁有足夠的電力，穩定的電力供應不會出現問題。

2. The coach was emphatic about the importance of teamwork. 教練非常強調團隊合作的重要性。

3. He gave an emphatic denial of the accusations against him. 他對針對他的指控給出了明確的否認。

同義詞與參考例句

1. Definite（明確的）
   She gave a definite answer to the question. 她對這個問題給出了明確的答案。

2. Assertive（堅定的）
   He was very assertive in his opinion. 他在他的觀點上非常堅定。

3. Unambiguous（明確的）

   This contract contains unambiguous terms and conditions. 這份合約包含明確的條款和條件。

4. Unequivocal（毫不含糊的）

   Her answer was unequivocal；she said yes without hesitation. 她的回答毫不含糊，她毫不猶豫地說了「是」。

5. Explicit（清晰的）

   The instructions were explicit, leaving no room for confusion. 這些指示非常清晰，不容易引起混淆。

6. Outright（明確的）

   He made it outright clear that he wouldn't tolerate any more mistakes. 他明確表示他不會再容忍任何錯誤。

7. Categorical（明確的）：The manager's categorical statement reassured the team. 經理明確的聲明讓團隊感到放心。

Enamor │ 迷戀到上癮

Enamor動詞，使某人或某物陷入愛情或迷戀之中。通常用於描述某人深深愛上另一人或事物的情感狀態。

Enamor的例句及應用：

1. He became enamored of her the moment he saw her across the room. 他一見到她，立刻就對她著迷了。
2. She was completely enamored with the idea of traveling the world. 她對環遊世界的想法完全迷戀不已。
3. The young artist was enamored with the beauty of nature, which inspired his paintings. 年輕藝術家對大自然的美麗深感著迷，這激發了他的畫作靈感。

Enamor的同義詞或相關詞彙及應用

1. Infatuate（動詞）：使某人陷入強烈的愛慕或著迷狀態。
   She quickly became infatuated with the charismatic actor. 她很快就對這位有魅力的演員著迷了。
2. Fascinate（動詞）：引起某人極大的興趣、好奇心或著迷。
   The mysterious ancient artifact fascinated archaeologists. 那個神祕的古代文物讓考古學家們感到著迷。
3. Captivate（動詞）：吸引某人的注意力、心靈或感情。
   The singer's enchanting voice captivated the entire audience.

歌手迷人的聲音迷住了整個觀眾。

4. Smitten（形容詞）：深深愛上或著迷的狀態。

He was utterly smitten with his new girlfriend. 他對他的新女朋友深深著迷。

5. Charmed（形容詞）：受到吸引或迷住的感覺。

She was charmed by the quaint beauty of the old town. 她對這個古老城鎮的別緻之處深感著迷。

以上這些詞彙都可以用來描述某人對某人、某物或某個概念產生深刻的情感或興趣，但程度和語境上有些微的不同。

Encumber｜阻礙／拖累

Encumber動詞，妨礙、阻礙、拖累或負擔。描述某物或某人對某事物的不利影響，使其變得更加困難或複雜。

來看一篇短文〈中國經濟的緩慢恢復拖累全球經濟〉：
The drastic sluggishness in the Chinese economy has sounded the alarm worldwide. Many European and American entrepreneurs warn that the slow recovery of the Chinese economy will encumber the global economy.
中國經濟的急劇放緩已經在全球敲響了警鐘。許多歐美企業家警告說，中國經濟的緩慢恢復將妨礙（拖累）全球經濟。

來看一下例句應用

1. The excessive paperwork encumbered the progress of the project, causing delays. 過多的文件工作妨礙了計劃的進展，導致了延誤。

2. Heavy debt can encumber a person's financial freedom for years. 沉重的債務可以妨礙一個人的財務自由多年。

3. The old, outdated software encumbered the efficiency of the computer system. 老舊的、過時的軟體妨礙了電腦系統的效率。

Encumber的同義字詞、片語

1. Hinder（妨礙、阻撓）

   The heavy workload can hinder productivity. 沉重的工作量可以妨礙生產力。

2. Impede（阻礙、阻止）

   English Sentence: The traffic jam impeded our journey to the airport. 交通堵塞阻礙了我們前往機場的行程。

3. Burdensome（繁重的、沉重的）

   The burdensome regulations made it difficult for small businesses to thrive. 繁重的法規使得小企業難以茁壯。

4. Obstruct（阻撓、阻礙）

   The fallen tree obstructed the path, making it impossible to pass. 倒下的樹阻礙了路徑，使得無法通行。

5. Cumber（妨礙、阻礙）

   Excessive paperwork can cumber the progress of a project. 過多的文件工作可以妨礙一個計劃的進展。

6. Hamper（阻礙）：用於描述使事情變得更困難或更緩慢。

   The heavy workload hampered their progress. 繁重的工作負荷阻礙了他們的進展。

7. Inhibit（抑制）：指阻止或限制某事的發展。

   Fear can inhibit creativity and innovation. 恐懼可以抑制創造力和創新。

8. Bog down（使陷入困境）：指將事情變得更加複雜或耗時。

   Excessive bureaucracy can bog down government processes. 過度的官僚主義會使政府流程受到阻礙。

Ennui | 倦怠感

Ennui名詞，「無聊厭倦」的感覺。

來看一下在短文中如何應用：

Most office workers have experienced moments of physical and mental exhaustion, where we often grit our teeth and push through. However, at times, no matter how much we endure or rest, the doctor suggests that we might be succumbing to ennui, a condition where life feels profoundly dull and indifferent, and the spark of motivation or enthusiasm has seemingly burned out.

大多數上班族都曾經歷過身體和心靈疲憊的時刻，我們經常咬緊牙關堅持下去。然而，有時，無論我們多麼忍受或休息，醫生建議我們可能正在陷入倦怠ennui，一種生活感覺極度乏味和冷漠的狀態，動力或熱情的火花似乎已經燃盡。

Ennui的例句應用

1. I experienced a deep sense of ennui during the long, monotonous meeting. 我在那場冗長單調的會議中感到深深的倦怠。

2. Her ennui with her job led her to seek new career opportunities. 她對工作感到倦怠，因此開始尋找新的職業機會。

3. The ennui of living in a small, quiet town eventually drove

him to move to the bustling city. 在一個小而寂靜的小鎮生活的倦怠最終讓他搬到了熙熙攘攘的城市。

4. To combat ennui, he took up a new hobby to fill his free time. 爲了對抗倦怠，他開始學習新的愛好來塡補閒暇時間。

Ennui的同義詞以及相應的例句

1. Boredom（無聊）

   She couldn't shake off the boredom of the long, rainy weekend. 她無法擺脫漫長、多雨的週末帶來的無聊感。

2. Tedium（乏味）

   The tedium of data entry made the job feel never-ending. 數據輸入的乏味使這份工作感覺永無止境。

3. Monotony（單調）

   The monotony of his daily routine was starting to wear on him. 他日常生活的單調開始讓他感到疲憊。

4. Weariness（疲倦）

   The long hike left them with a sense of weariness. 長途徒步讓他們感到疲倦。

5. Apathy（冷漠）

   His constant apathy towards social issues was concerning. 他對社會問題的持續冷漠令人擔憂。

6. Fatigue（疲勞）

   After a long day of work, she felt a deep sense of fatigue. 在一天的工作之後，她感到極度的疲勞。

7. Listless（倦怠）

   His listless attitude towards his studies was concerning to his parents. 他對學業的倦怠態度讓他的父母感到擔憂。

8. Lassitude（無力）

The heat wave left everyone with a sense of lassitude. 熱浪讓每個人都感到無力。

9. Languor（懶散）

The languor of a lazy summer afternoon was palpable. 懶散的夏日午後的懶散感讓人感受到。

10. Sluggishness（遲鈍）

The sluggishness of the computer frustrated the user. 電腦的遲鈍讓用戶感到沮喪。

11. Enervation（無力）

The illness resulted in a state of enervation that lasted for weeks. 這種疾病導致了數周的無力感。

12. Melancholy（憂鬱）

The rainy, gray day filled her with a sense of melancholy. 陰雨綿綿的一天讓她感到憂鬱。

13. Despondency（絕望）

His repeated failures led to a deep sense of despondency. 他屢次失敗使他感到深深的絕望。

這些詞彙都可以描述與Ennui類似的情感，但每個詞彙可能有其獨特的意境和細微差異。Ennui強調無聊、倦怠及冷漠，而Despondency則更強調絕望。

Estrange | 疏離／疏遠

Estrange動詞，使某人或某事物變得陌生、疏遠或不親近。用於描述人際關係或情感的變化，使關係變得疏遠或不和睦。

短文中可以這樣運用Estrange：

The media reports that Ai Fukuhara's（福原愛）brother, who used to offer both public and private support to Ai Fukuhara, had a strong bond with her. However, they have now dissolved the companies they both invested in, and the reports state, Ai Fukuhara's brother feels that their relationship has become increasingly estranged.

媒體報導福原愛的哥哥過去於公於私支持福原愛許多，兄妹倆感情深厚，如今卻解散了彼此都投資的公司，報導表示：「福原愛的哥哥覺得兄妹倆的關係也變得越來越疏遠。

以下是應用的英文例句

1. The constant arguments and lack of communication began to estrange the once-close friends. 不斷的爭吵和缺乏溝通開始使曾經親近的朋友感到疏遠。

2. Years of living abroad can sometimes estrange you from your native culture. 多年在國外生活有時會使你與你的本土文化疏遠。

3. His secretive behavior began to estrange him from his family, as they no longer trusted him. 他的神祕行爲開始使他與家人疏遠，因爲他們不再信任他。

Estrange的同義詞及應用的例句

1. Alienate疏遠

   His constant criticism of her work began to alienate her from the team. 他對她工作的不斷批評開始使她與團隊疏遠。
2. Distance拉開距離（動詞）

   The long-distance relationship started to distance them emotionally.這段遠距離關係開始在情感上拉開距離。
3. Separate分離

   Their conflicting beliefs and values eventually separated them. 他們相互衝突的信仰和價值觀最終使他們分道揚鑣。」
4. Estrangement疏遠

   The estrangement between the two siblings was heartbreaking for their parents. 兩兄妹之間的疏遠對他們的父母來說，是令人心碎的。
5. Isolate孤立／遠離

   His decision to isolate himself from social gatherings led to a sense of estrangement. 他決定遠離社交聚會的決定導致了一種疏遠感。

其他與Estrange近似的同義字詞、片語

1. Antagonize：引起敵對情緒或行爲，對某人或某事持挑釁或對抗的態度。

His constant criticism seemed to antagonize his coworkers, making the workplace tense. 他不斷批評似乎激怒了他的同事，使工作場所變得緊張。

2. Sow discord：散布不和或不和諧的情感，故意在群體中種下分歧或不合的種子。

The malicious gossip was intended to sow discord among the friends. 那惡意的八卦意圖在朋友之間散播不和。

3. Sow dissension：散布分歧或不合，類似sow discord，強調在群體中引發不同意見或紛爭。

Their divisive comments were meant to sow dissension within the team. 他們的分裂性評論旨在團隊內引起分歧。

Antagonize、Sow discord和Sow dissension 和Estrange有相似之處，但它們各自強調不同方面的關係破裂或疏遠。

Ethereal ｜ 空靈系

Ethereal形容詞，非常精緻、非現實的、超凡脫俗的、空靈的感覺，常用來形容像夢境般的、極爲美麗或不眞實的事物。

A singer has a weirdly ethereal voice 一位擁有奇特超凡脫俗嗓音的歌手。

Ethereal幾個例句

1. The music at the cathedral was ethereal, creating a sense of transcendence. 大教堂的音樂非常空靈，營造出一種超凡的感覺。

2. The ethereal beauty of the sunrise over the ocean took my breath away.大海上日出的超凡脫俗之美讓我嘆爲觀止

3. The music at the concert was so ethereal that it felt like we were transported to another world. 那場音樂會的音樂如此空靈，讓我們感覺好像被帶到了另一個世界。

4. Her voice had an ethereal quality, like a whisper from a distant dream. 她的聲音具有空靈的特質，就像來自遙遠夢境的低語。

5. The mist rising from the lake gave the landscape an ethereal and otherworldly appearance. 從湖面升起的薄霧賦予了這片風景一種空靈而超凡脫俗的外貌。

與Ethereal同義的字及例子

1. Celestial（天上的）：屬於天堂或天空的，形容某物神聖非凡。

   The stars in the night sky have a celestial beauty. 夜空中的星星有著天上的美麗。

2. Transcendent（卓越的）：表示超越常人或世俗，具有卓越的品質或性質。

   His talent in music is truly transcendent; it touches the soul. 他在音樂方面的天賦真的非常卓越，觸動了靈魂。

3. Otherworldly（超凡的）：描述某物超出尋常，似乎來自另一個世界。

   The landscape of the alien planet looked completely otherworldly. 外星球的風景看起來完全超凡脫俗。

4. Divine（神聖的）：與神或神性相關聯的，具有神聖的性質。

   The temple's architecture had a divine elegance that left visitors in awe. 寺廟的建築具有神聖的優雅，讓遊客感到敬畏。

5. Spiritual（精神的）：表示某物與精神或靈性有關聯，形容超自然的體驗或感覺。

   Meditation can lead to a deep, spiritual connection with oneself. 冥想可以帶來與自己深刻的精神連結。

Graceful、Delicate、Exquisite和Ethereal有一些相似之處，在意義上些微不同

1. Graceful（優雅的）：形容某物或某人有著優美、優雅的

風格或動作。

The ballet dancer's movements were incredibly graceful. 芭蕾舞者的動作非常優雅。

2. Delicate（精緻的）：形容某物具有精緻、細緻的特點，通常指物體脆弱或需要小心對待。

She held the delicate porcelain teacup with great care. 她小心翼翼地拿著精緻的瓷茶杯。

3. Exquisite（精緻的）：與Delicate類似，形容某物非常精巧、優美，通常用來形容工藝、設計或細節。

The chef prepared an exquisite dish with intricate flavors. 廚師烹製了一道精緻的菜肴，口味繁複。

Facile. | 輕而易舉

Facile形容詞，容易的、輕而易舉的。描述事情容易或過於簡單的情境下使用。

來閱讀一篇短文，如何將Facile應用在〈讀醫學系容易交女友的說法與現實〉中：

A Dcard user expressed their astonishment at the stark contrast between hearing that studying medicine makes it easy to find a girlfriend and the reality of their situation, which they found to be facile. They shared that looks and personality are significant factors influencing one's success in dating and cautioned against the misconception that entering medical school automatically upgrades all other aspects of one's life. The user's experience serves as a reminder for others to think more carefully about these aspects.

一位Dcard網友表示對於聽到讀醫學系容易交女友的說法與現實情況之間的鮮明對比感到傻眼，他們認爲情況「輕而易舉」。他們指出外貌和個性是影響約會成功的重要因素，並警告不要誤以爲進入醫學院會自動提升生活的其他方面。這位網友的經驗提醒其他人更謹愼地思考這些方面。

來看看幾個例句

1. The puzzle was so facile that my five-year-old nephew solved

it in minutes. 這個拼圖如此容易，我的五歲侄子幾分鐘就解決了。

2. Her facile understanding of mathematics made her the top student in the class. 她對數學的輕鬆理解使她成爲班上的尖子生。

3. The chef's facile preparation of the meal left everyone impressed with his skills. 廚師輕而易舉地準備了這頓餐，讓每個人對他的技藝印象深刻。

Facile的同義詞，以及例句

1. 容易的（Easy）

Learning to ride a bicycle is easy for most children. 對大多數兒童來說，學騎自行車是容易的。

2. 簡單的（Simple）

The instructions for assembling the furniture were simple to follow. 組裝家具的說明非常簡單。

3. 順利的（Smooth）

The project went smoothly thanks to effective teamwork. 多虧了有效的團隊合作，這個專案進展順利。

4. 輕而易舉的（Effortless）

For her, solving complex math problems is effortless. 對她來說，解決複雜的數學問題是輕而易舉的。

5. 順心如意的（Cakewalk）

Passing that exam was a cakewalk for him; he had studied diligently. 通過那個考試對他來說輕而易舉；他曾刻苦學習。

Fester ｜惡化

Fester惡化、Rankle激怒、canker潰瘍、Ulcerate潰爛這四個字與傷口、激怒與惡化有關，但有細微差別：

1. Fester（潰爛）指的是傷口或感染部位因細菌滋生而逐漸惡化或變糟。

2. Rankle（激怒；激起怨恨）不僅可以指肉體上的疼痛，還可以指情感上的不滿或怨恨，通常是某種困擾或惱怒的情感。

3. Canker（潰瘍）是一種潰爛性的傷口，通常出現在黏膜或軟組織上，例如口腔潰瘍。

4. Ulcerate（潰爛）是一個廣泛的術語，用於形容組織或皮膚表面的傷口或潰爛。

每個詞語應用的例句

1. Fester（惡化、潰爛）

Without proper care, the wound began to fester and became infected. 如果不得到適當的護理，傷口會開始潰爛並感染。

2. Rankle（激怒；激起怨恨）

The unfair treatment she received continued to rankle in her mind, making it difficult for her to forgive and forget. 她所受到的不公平待遇持續激起她的不滿，讓她難以原諒和忘記。

The lingering resentment between the two families had rankled for generations, leading to a bitter feud. 兩個家庭之間持續存在的怨恨已經存在了幾代人，導致了一場激烈的仇恨。

3. Canker（潰瘍）

Mouth ulcers, also known as canker sores, can be quite painful. 口腔潰瘍，也被稱為潰爛性潰瘍，可能相當疼痛。

4. Ulcerate（潰爛）

If left untreated, the infection can cause the wound to ulcerate and worsen. 如果不治療，感染可能會導致傷口潰爛和惡化。

Fester也可以指情感、問題或困擾逐漸惡化或積壓，像是⋯

1. The unresolved issues between the two countries continued to fester, leading to increased tensions. 兩國之間未解決的問題持續惡化，導致緊張局勢升級。

2. Her resentment began to fester, poisoning her relationships with those around her. 她的憤恨開始積壓，毒害了她與周圍人的關係。

3. Ignoring a small problem can allow it to fester into a much larger and more difficult one. 忽視一個小問題可能會讓它漸變成（惡化）為一個更大更難處理的問題。

5 Laws Of Life and their relation to embrace success.

五大心理學及生活法則,看懂「墨菲定律」、「吉德林特法則」、「吉爾伯特法則」、「沃爾森法則」、「福克蘭法則」。一起來看懂頂級思維,駕馭人生。

Murphy's law

The more you fear something, the more it will happen. 如果你害怕某事,它更有可能發生。這個法則暗示著焦慮和恐懼可能會影響人們的行為,使他們更容易遭遇他們害怕的情況。

Kidlin law

If you can write down the problem clearly, it is half solved. 如果你能清晰地將問題寫下來,那麼解決問題的一半已經完成。這強調了問題定義和清晰思考的重要性。將問題清楚地表達出來有助於更容易找到解決方案。

Gilbert law

The biggest problem at work is that none tells you what to do. 工作中大問題是沒有人告訴你該做什麼。意思是說人生危險的事,是沒人跟你談危險,如果自己蠻幹只是畫地自限的井底之蛙,一切只看到平面,沒有立體透徹的了解,只會徒增

困擾及危險。

Walson law

If you keep putting information and intelligence first at all the time, money keeps coming in. 如果你一直把資訊和智慧放在首位，錢就會持續流入。這個法則暗示了知識經濟在管理的價值，可能有助於取得經濟上的成就。

Falkland Law

When there is no need to make a decision, Don't make a decision. Save that brain space for something more important. 當沒有必要做出決策時，不要做出決策。這個法則強調了選擇的重要性，節省精力和資源，不必要的決策可能會浪費時間和精力的浪費。

這些「法則」是基於觀察和經驗值提出的一些原則，並非學術性質心或公認的原則，在實際應用中，每個法則的效果取決於自身情境和個人特質，希望對大家有所幫助。

Flake on │ 被放鴿子

Flake on指某人計劃好的事情或承諾後來無法兌現，通常是因爲他們失約或不履行承諾。這表示他們對原來的計劃或約定不負責任，就是「被放鴿子」的意思。

來看看Flake on運用的範例

1. He flaked on our dinner date last night, and I had to eat alone. 他昨晚失約了，我不得不獨自吃飯。

2. Don't be the kind of person who always flakes on their friends when they make plans. 別成爲那種朋友約好了計劃卻總是失約、放人鴿子的人。

3. She promised to help with the project, but she flaked on us at the last minute. 她答應幫忙這個計畫，但她在最後一刻食言了。

與Flake on類似含義的單字和片語

1. Bail on：在約定或計劃之前突然取消或放棄。
   She bailed on the movie night we had planned. 她取消了我們計劃好的看電影之夜。

2. Stand someone up：在約會或約定中，一方突然不來或遲到。
   He stood me up at the restaurant last night. 昨晚他在餐廳放我鴿子。

3. Back out：在事前撤回或取消承諾。

   She backed out of the agreement at the last minute. 她在最後一刻取消了協議。

Flamboyant
｜引人矚目／光彩奪目

Flamboyant形容人或物體表現出極端引人注目、奪目和華麗的特徵，通常伴隨著自信、活潑和炫耀的風格。描述個人風格、服裝、行為或表演，以突顯其非常引人注目和有吸引力的特點。

Each year, various fireworks festivals around the world, masterfully orchestrated by pyrotechnic experts, transform the night into a flamboyantly colorful and dazzlingly beautiful spectacle.

每年各地的煙火節由煙火大師精心操刀，讓黑夜變得繽紛多彩，呈現出光彩奪目且極具特色的美麗景象。

Flamboyant的例句

1. Her flamboyant sense of fashion always turns heads at social events. 她極具華麗時尚感的穿著總是在社交活動中吸引眾人的注目。

2. The actor's flamboyant performance on stage captivated the audience's attention from the beginning to the end. 這位演員在舞台上極富炫耀性的表演從頭到尾都吸引了觀眾的注意力。

3. The flamboyant decorations at the carnival created a festive

and lively atmosphere. 遊樂會上的華麗裝飾營造出節日和熱鬧的氛圍。

Flamboyant的同義詞以及例子

1. Dazzling（形容詞）：意思是極其耀眼、令人眼花繚亂的。

   The fireworks display was truly dazzling, lighting up the night sky. 煙火表演眞的非常耀眼，照亮了夜空。

2. Showy（形容詞）：指引人注目、炫耀或華麗的。

   Her showy jewelry collection is the envy of many. 她華麗的珠寶收藏令許多人嫉妒。

3. Extravagant（形容詞）：意指極度奢華或浪費的。

   The ballroom was decorated with extravagant floral arrangements. 舞廳裝飾著奢華的花卉布置。

4. Opulent（形容詞）：描述非常富裕、奢華或豪華的事物。

   The opulent palace was a symbol of the king's wealth and power. 這座奢華的宮殿是國王財富和權力的象徵。

5. Ostentatious（形容詞）：指刻意炫耀或爲了吸引注意而不自然的。

   His ostentatious display of wealth included expensive cars and lavish parties. 他刻意炫耀財富，包括昂貴的汽車和奢華的派對。

Flummox │ 困惑

Flummox動詞，困惑、迷惑、使混亂。通常在當某人或某事情使人感到困惑、不知所措時使用。

以下為例句及應用

1. The unexpected twist in the plot completely flummoxed the audience, leaving them in awe. 劇情中出現的意外轉折完全讓觀眾感到困惑，讓他們感到驚嘆。

2. The complex instructions flummoxed the new employees, leaving them unsure of what to do. 複雜的指示使新員工感到困惑，讓他們不確定該做什麼。

3. Her detailed explanation of the scientific theory left me utterly flummoxed; I couldn't grasp a word of it. 她對科學理論的詳細解釋讓我完全感到困惑，我一句話都不懂。

Flummox的同義詞以及例句

1. Baffle（困惑）：To confuse or perplex someone.
   The complicated math problem baffled the students. 這個複雜的數學問題讓學生感到困惑。

2. Bewilder（迷惑）：To cause someone to become puzzled or confused.
   The sudden change in plans bewildered her. 計畫的突然變化讓她感到迷惑。

FancyEnglish 精湛英文

3. Confound（混淆）：To cause surprise or confusion by acting against expectations.

His ability to speak five languages confounded everyone at the conference. 他能說五種語言讓會議上的每個人都感到困惑。

4. Perplex（使困惑）：To cause someone to be puzzled or confused.

The complex instructions perplexed the participants. 複雜的指示使參與者感到困惑。

這些同義詞描述了使人感到困惑、混亂或迷惑的情況，它們可以在不同語境中用來代替flummox。

Palsy-Walsy｜友善

Palsy-walsy的同義字有amicable、affable。

與媒體間保持友善關係可以這樣表達：The government and the press have a palsy-walsy relationship⋯

閱讀一篇有關「與我國友好國家在聯合國為台灣仗義執言」的短文，學習如何應用這個詞彙：

In recent times, a number of countries with palsy-walsy relations with our nation have been stepping up their efforts at the United Nations to speak up for Taiwan. They firmly believe that Taiwan should not be left in international isolation. Their stance underscores the importance of inclusivity and cooperation on the global stage, where Taiwan's meaningful participation can contribute to addressing pressing global issues.

近年來，一些與我友好關係的國家一直在聯合國加大努力，積極為台灣發聲。他們堅信台灣不應該在國際上孤立無援。他們的立場強調了全球舞台上包容性和合作的重要性，台灣的有意義參與可以有助於應對迫切的全球問題。

例句

1. The team's palsy-walsy relationship creates a warm atmosphere, fostering a strong sense of solidarity. 團隊中友好的關係營造了一種溫暖的氛圍，培養了強烈的團結意識。

2. The political figure appeared his palsy-walsy on the platform, making audience feel as if they were old pals. 這位政治人物在講台上表現得很親民友善，讓觀眾們覺得就像是老朋友一樣。

Frivolous | 輕浮

Frivolous形容詞，輕浮的、不嚴肅的、草率的。用來形容行為或言談缺乏認真或重要性的情境。

例句

1. He was criticized for his frivolous attitude during the important business meeting. 他在重要的商務會議上因其輕浮的態度而受到批評。
2. Her frivolous spending habits left her in financial trouble. 她不謹慎的花費習慣讓她陷入了財務困境。
3. Making jokes about such a serious topic is quite frivolous. 對於如此嚴肅的話題開玩笑是相當不合適的。

Frivolous表示某人或某事缺乏適當的認真態度或重要性，常常用來批評不負責任、不認真的行為或言談。

其他輕率或不認真意思的字詞如下

1. Frolicsome（形容詞）：表示某人或某物活潑、快樂、喜歡嬉戲的性格。用來描述playful或joyous的情境。
   The children were in a frolicsome mood as they played in the park. 孩子們在公園裡嬉戲，情緒高昂。
2. Flippant（形容詞）：表示某人輕率、不認真，通常涉及對重要或嚴肅事物的不適當對待。

FancyEnglish 精湛英文

His flippant comments during the meeting offended some of the participants. 他在會議中的輕率評論冒犯了一些參與者。

3. Giddy（形容詞）：表示某人感到頭昏眼花、充滿興奮或混亂，通常涉及情感或生理狀態。

   She felt giddy with excitement when she won the competition. 當她贏得比賽時，她感到興奮得頭昏眼花。

4. Frivolous（形容詞）：與前三者有些相似，表示不認真、輕浮，但通常更強調缺乏重要性或價值。

   Making jokes about the tragedy was seen as a frivolous response. 對於這個悲劇開玩笑被視為一種不重視的反應。

上述這些詞語都有輕率的意思，但使用情境和語境可以區分。Frolicsome通常描述開心、愉快的情境，而flippant不當態度地對待重要事物，giddy則強調情感或生理狀態上的快速變化，而frivolous則是輕浮的意思。

Fungible
| 可互相替代的資產或物品

Fungible表示某些東西可以被交換或替代，不會有實質差異。在許多情況下，用於在數值和品質上是相同的貨幣或商品，因此可以互相交換。

可以替代Fungible的詞語

Interchangeable（可互換的）、Replaceable（可替代的）、
Commutable（可交換的）

應用例句

1. Gold bars are considered fungible because each bar is of the same weight and purity. 金條被認為是可互換的，因為金條的重量和純度都相同。

2. In the stock market, shares of the same company are typically fungible and can be freely traded. 在股票市場中，同一家公司的股票通常是可互換的，可以自由交易。

3. One-dollar bills are fungible, meaning you can exchange one for another without any difference in value. 一美元鈔票是可互換的，你可以互換一張和另一張，其價值不會有任何差異。

4. In a digital wallet, one bitcoin is fungible with another. 在數位錢包中，一個比特幣可以與另一個互換。

FancyEnglish 精湛英文

Genteel | 優雅／文雅

Genteel形容詞，有教養的、有禮貌的，形容某人或某物的風格或舉止是優雅、文雅、不粗俗的。

例句及翻譯

1. She has a genteel manner about her that makes everyone feel comfortable in her presence. 她的舉止文雅，讓每個人在她身旁都感到舒適。

2. The genteel atmosphere of the Victorian-era tea party was characterized by elaborate etiquette and refined conversation. 維多利亞時代茶會的文雅氛圍以精緻的禮儀和優美的對話爲特點。

3. The genteel architecture of the neighborhood reflected its rich history and sophisticated residents. 這個地區的文雅建築反映了其悠久的歷史和有教養的居民。

Genteel的同義字

1. Polite（有禮貌的）：有禮貌，遵循社會規範。
   She always speaks in a polite manner. 她總是以有禮貌的方式講話。

2. Refined（優雅的）：有教養和精緻，高雅的。
   The refined decor of the restaurant creates a pleasant atmosphere. 餐廳精緻的裝飾營造出愉悅的氛圍

3. Elegant（優雅的）：高雅的，優美的。

   She wore an elegant gown to the gala.她穿著一件優雅的禮服參加了晚會。

4. Sophisticated（老練的）：富有經驗和品味，精通世故的。

   He has a sophisticated taste in art.他對藝術有著老練的品味。

5. Cultured（有教養的）：具有教育和文化修養的。

   She is a cultured woman who appreciates classical music. 她是一位有教養的女士，喜歡古典音樂。

6. Civilized（文明的）：有文化的，遵循文明標準的。

   Living in a civilized society requires respecting the rights of others.在文明社會中生活需要尊重他人的權利。

這些詞語都可以用來描述有禮貌、優雅和文化修養的特質，它們在不同上下文中可以互換使用。

有相似之處，但在意思上有區別的字彙

1. Exquisite（精緻）通常指的是具有卓越的美麗、優雅或精湛的品質。它經常用來描述藝術、工藝或精美的餐飲。

   The jewelry was exquisite in its design and craftsmanship. 這件珠寶的設計和工藝都非常精緻。

2. Decent（體面的）通常表示符合社會接受的行為或道德標準。它可以描述某事物是可敬的、公平的或適當的。

   He always behaved in a decent manner, treating everyone with respect. 他總是以體面的方式行事，尊重每個人。

3. Good-mannered（有禮貌的）指的是表現出禮貌和良好行為的人。它關注擁有良好的禮儀並且考慮他人感受。

She is a good-mannered young lady who is always polite to others. 她是一位有禮貌的年輕女士，總是對他人禮貌。

Glower | 怒視

Glower：Have an angry or sullen look，動詞，怒視或怒氣沖沖地凝視，通常表示不滿、生氣或敵意。

一則新聞案例中「首位前美國總統在面對刑事指控時以怒視表情被攝影的第一人」，我們可以這樣運用：

President Trump, facing legal charges for his attempts to overturn the 2020 presidential election, was granted bail by the court but still glowered at the camera with a lowered forehead. This image was captured and would go down in history as the first former U.S. president to be photographed with a glowering expression while facing criminal charges.

川普總統因試圖推翻2020年總統選舉而面臨法律指控，雖然法庭裁定保釋，但他仍然怒視鏡頭，皺著眉頭。這一畫面被拍攝下來，將成為歷史上首位前美國總統在面對刑事指控時以怒視表情被攝影的第一人。

其他Glower應用的例句

1. He couldn't hide his annoyance and began to glower at his colleague who had interrupted the meeting. 他無法掩飾自己的惱怒，開始對那位打斷會議的同事怒視著。

2. The teacher glowered at the students who were talking loudly in class, making them immediately quiet down. 老師怒視著

在課堂上大聲談笑的學生，讓他們立刻安靜下來。

3. As the argument escalated, their faces contorted in anger, and they began to glower at each other, making the tension in the room palpable. 隨著爭論升級，他們的臉上充斥著憤怒，開始怒視對方，使房間的緊張氛圍變得明顯。

和Glower類似情境的同義字

1. Frown（皺眉）

She gave him a stern frown when he arrived late. 當他遲到時，她臉上浮現出一個嚴厲的皺眉。

2. Scowl（皺眉）

He scowled at the bad news he received. 他對收到的壞消息皺起了眉頭。

3. Glare（怒視）

The teacher glared at the students who were talking during the lecture. 老師怒視那些在講座期間交談的學生。

4. Sneer（嗤之以鼻）

She sneered at his feeble excuse for not completing the assignment. 她對他草率的辯解完成作業的理由嗤之以鼻。

5. Grimace（扭曲表情）

He grimaced in pain when he stubbed his toe. 當他踢到腳趾時，他因疼痛而扭曲了表情。

6. Look daggers（以敵意或威脅性的眼神來示意或表達不滿）

She looked daggers at her coworker for taking credit for her idea. 對同事為她的點子而獲得功勞感到憤怒，用充滿敵

意的眼神瞪著她。

7. Stare angrily（生氣地盯著）

He stared angrily at the traffic jam outside his window. 他生氣地盯著窗外的交通堵塞。

Goof around｜嬉鬧

Don't goof around! 小心老闆就在你背後別在打混了，Goof around是口語用語，通常指某人在某種情境下做愚蠢、無聊或不負責任的事情，而不是專注或認真對待事情。

來看一下例句

1. Stop goofing around and finish your homework! 別再亂來，把你的作業完成！
2. They spent the afternoon goofing around at the park instead of studying for the exam. 他們整個下午都在公園裡瞎鬧，而不是準備考試。
3. The boss doesn't like it when employees goof around during office hours. 老板不喜歡員工在上班時間玩忽職守。

一些和Goof around類似的英語用語

1. Mess around：浪費時間，或者做一些較不重要、愚蠢或不負責任的事情。
   Instead of studying for the exam, they chose to mess around and play video games. 他們選擇打電動，而不是讀書準備考試，真是浪費時間。
2. Horse around：做幼稚、愚蠢或不負責任的事情，通常伴隨著嬉鬧和開玩笑。
   The kids were horsing around in the backyard, laughing and

chasing each other. 孩子們在後院嬉鬧，笑聲不斷，互相追逐。

3. Act silly：表現愚蠢或嬉鬧，通常在輕鬆的情境下。

They decided to act silly and wear funny costumes for the costume party. 他們決定在化妝派對上裝扮得很滑稽。

4. Goof off：偷懶或浪費時間，指在工作或學業上不認真對待。

Instead of doing their assignments, they chose to goof off and watch TV all day. 他們選擇偷懶，整天看電視，而不是做作業。

這些俚語和片語都描述了一種較不認真、愚蠢或輕鬆的行為，通常在非正式的情境中使用。

Goof around和Loiter around的不同之處

1. Goof around：玩樂或嬉戲，通常是輕鬆和愉快的活動，可能帶有一點幽默成分。

He spent the afternoon goofing around with his friends at the park. 他花了下午和朋友在公園嬉戲玩耍。

2. Loiter around：在某處閒逛或徘徊，通常帶有一種目的不明確或無所作為的感覺，可能會引起不必要的注意或被視為打擾。

The security guard told the teenagers not to loiter around the mall entrance. 保安告訴那些青少年不要在購物中心入口閒逛。

Goof around可以翻譯為「嬉戲玩耍」。

Loiter around可以翻譯為「閒逛徘徊」。

Hound vs Pester
糾纏 vs 追逐

1. Pester纏擾、糾纏

動詞，當某人一再打擾或糾纏另一人或希望得到某種回應時，可以使用。

1. She pestered her brother to borrow his car for the weekend.
   她糾纏她的兄弟，想借他的車過週末。
2. The persistent salesperson pestered me with phone calls every day. 這位固執的銷售員每天都用電話不停地糾纏我。
3. Please stop pestering the teacher with so many questions during class. 上課時請不要再一直問老師那麼多問題。

2. Hound追逐、不斷追問

動詞，當某人追逐某物或某人，或者不斷地追問某人某事，可以使用。

1. The detective hounded the suspect all night to gather evidence. 這名偵探整晚追蹤嫌疑犯以收集證據。
2. The media hounded the celebrity for comments on the recent scandal. 媒體不斷追問這位名人對最近的醜聞有什麼評論。
3. He hounds his coworkers with questions about the project's progress. 他不停地向同事追問有關專案進展的問題。

Pester的同義字和例句

Pester（騷擾）的同義字有：annoy、bother、harass、irritate、nag、molest等。

1. Pester：持續或重複地打擾、煩擾或困擾他人，通常是因為不斷地提問、要求或干擾。

   She would always pester her brother with questions when he was trying to study. 她總是在她兄弟試圖學習時糾纏不休地問問題。

2. Annoy（惱怒）：引起某人輕微的不悅或煩惱，通常是由令人討厭、刺激或不斷發生的事情引起。

   His constant tapping on the desk started to annoy his coworkers. 他不斷敲打桌子的行為開始讓他的同事感到惱怒。

3. Bother（打擾）：引起不便或煩擾某人，可能需要花費時間或精力來處理。

   I didn't want to bother you, but I have a question about the project. 我不想打擾你，但我對這個專案有個問題。

4. Harass（騷擾）：不斷地困擾、迫害或煩擾他人，通常是有目的地對其施加壓力或威脅。

   She filed a complaint against her coworker for sexually harassing her at the office. 她對她的同事在辦公室對她進行性騷擾提出了投訴。

5. Irritate（刺激／激怒）：引起某人的不耐煩、憤怒或不滿，通常是由惱人或令人不快的事物引起。

   The constant noise from the construction site irritated the residents of the neighborhood. 建築工地不斷的噪音讓附近

居民感到惱怒。

6. Molest（騷擾／侵犯）：不法地、不當地騷擾、侵犯或傷害某人，通常涉及性或身體上的侵害。

He was arrested for molesting a minor, and now he faces serious legal consequences. 他因對未成年人進行侵犯而被捕，現在面臨嚴重的法律後果。

7. Nag（嘮叨／糾纏）：表不斷地給某人提建議、批評或要求，通常是煩人地糾纏或嘮叨。

She would constantly nag her husband to fix the leaky faucet in the kitchen. 她總是不停地嘮叨她的丈夫去修理廚房的漏水水龍頭。

Hound的同義字

1. Hound：在這個情境下指的是追逐或不斷地追問某人或某物，可能是出於好奇、需求或追求。

The paparazzi would hound the celebrity everywhere she went, trying to get a photo. 狗仔隨時跟蹤這名名人，試圖拍到她的照片。

2. Chase（追逐）：追趕、追逐某人或某物，為了接近或抓住它。

The police chased the suspect through the crowded streets. 警察穿越擁擠的街道追捕嫌疑犯。

3. Pursue（追求）：積極地追求、尋找、或追蹤某人或某事物，為了達到特定的目標或實現某種目的。

She decided to pursue a career in medicine and enrolled in medical school. 她決定追求醫學事業，並入讀醫學院。

4. Follow（跟隨）：跟隨某人或某事物的行動、路線或指示，通常出於順從或想要了解更多。

   The detective followed the suspect discreetly to gather evidence. 偵探悄悄地跟隨嫌疑犯以收集證據。

5. Trail（跟蹤／蹤）：祕密地或輕蔑地跟蹤、追蹤某人，為了監視其行動或活動。

   The journalist trailed the politician to uncover his hidden meetings. 記者跟蹤政治家，以揭露他的祕密會議。

6. Extort（勒索）：透過威脅、脅迫或敲詐某人來強行獲取財物、金錢或其他價值物品。

   The criminal tried to extort money from the business owner by threatening to harm his family. 罪犯試圖通過威脅傷害商業主的家人來敲詐錢財。

Infatuated │ 迷戀／痴迷

動詞,迷戀、熱戀、痴迷某些活動或事物。

來看一段「小賈斯汀熱」(Bieber Fever)在短文中如何應用 Infatuate:

Fans of Justin Bieber, known as Beliebers, are aficionados who obsessively adore him to the point of losing self-control. Their infatuation with him has deeply embedded itself in their minds. Neuroscientist Dr. Levin from McGill University in Canada has delved into researching this inexplicable idol phenomenon. Shockingly, he has stated that the global Bieber Fever is, in fact, a form of illness.

粉絲們對Justin Bieber重度迷戀到無法自我控制,而且對他的癡迷已經深深嵌入腦中,加拿大馬吉爾大學神經科學家萊維汀對於這股不思議的偶像浪潮投入研究,他竟語出驚人地表示,在全球掀起的「小賈斯汀熱」(Bieber Fever)其實是一種病。(註:Inexplicable 無法解釋或無法理解的。)

其他的用法示例

1. She became infatuated with her coworker after their first meeting. 她在第一次見面後就迷戀上了她的同事。
2. His infatuation with sports cars led him to spend all his savings on a new Ferrari. 他對跑車的熱愛使他花光了所有

的儲蓄買了一輛法拉利。

3. Don't infatuate yourself with material possessions; there's more to life than that. 不要迷戀於物質財富，生活還有更多內涵。

Infatuate通常用來描述一種強烈但可能是暫時的愛慕或迷戀情感，常常是不理性或過度的情感。

Infatuate的同義詞以及例句

1. Enamor迷戀（動詞）

   She quickly became enamored with the charming musician. 她很快就迷戀上那位迷人的音樂家。

2. Besotted著迷的（形容詞／動詞過去分詞）

   He was absolutely besotted with his new girlfriend. 他對新女朋友完全著迷。

3. Smitten吸引（動詞過去分詞）

   Sarah was smitten by his kindness and sense of humor. 莎拉被他的善良和幽默感所吸引。

4. Captivated吸引

   The audience was captivated by the actor's brilliant performance. 觀眾被演員精彩的表演所吸引。

5. Infatuated痴迷

   He was infatuated with the idea of traveling the world. 他痴迷於周遊世界的念頭。

這些詞都可以用來描述某人對某事或某人感到極度吸引或著

迷的情感，通常伴隨著強烈的情感和注意力。

與Infatuate相似但不完全相同的單字

1. Obsess著迷、沉迷：指對特定主題或問題不健康的持續關注。

   He would obsess over every detail of his artwork, striving for perfection. 他會著迷於自己藝術品的每個細節，追求完美。

2. Lovestruck愛戀的：因愛而感到極度著迷或陷入愛情的情感。

   She was lovestruck when she first laid eyes on him at the party. 她在派對上第一次看到他時就愛得神魂顛倒。

Infirmity │ 身體虛弱／不健康

Old age and infirmity come to men and women alike 年老和虛弱同樣降臨在男性和女性身上。

Infirmity的應用在文章中可以這樣表達：

During BLACKPINK's Melbourne world tour concert, member Jennie had to leave the stage midway due to an infirmity. YG Entertainment, their management company, later issued an official statement pledging to do their utmost to assist Jennie in her recovery, while she personally expressed her apologies to the fans. 在BLACKPINK的墨爾本世界巡迴演唱會中，成員Jennie因身體虛弱唱到一半不得不離開舞台。所屬經紀公司YG娛樂後來發布了一份官方聲明，承諾將盡最大努力協助Jennie恢復健康，而Jennie本人向粉絲表達了她的道歉之情。

來看看Infirmity的應用例句

1. His infirmity prevented him from participating in the marathon. 他的虛弱使他無法參加馬拉松賽。
2. The elderly are more susceptible to infirmities as they age. 年長者隨著年齡增長更容易患上身體不健康的問題。
3. Despite her infirmity, she maintained a positive outlook on life. 儘管她身體不健康，她仍保持著對生活的積極態度。

Infirmity的同義詞及例子

1. Weakness（虛弱）

   His illness left him with a profound weakness. 他的疾病使他變得非常虛弱。

2. Frailty（脆弱）

   The frailty of old age became evident in her movements. 老年的脆弱在她的動作中變得明顯。

3. Ailment（疾病）

   She suffered from various ailments in her later years. 她在晚年患有各種疾病。

這邊要特別把這個單字拿出來的別解釋，Susceptible意思是容易受到某種影響、感染，通常用來形容一個人、事物或情況。

來看看Susceptible的例句及應用

1. He is susceptible to the flu virus, so he always stays vigilant. 他對感冒病毒很容易感染，因此總是保持警惕。

2. This plant is susceptible to damage in dry conditions. 這種植物在乾燥的環境下很容易受損。

3. Children are a susceptible group to negative influences on social media. 孩子們是社交媒體上不良影響的易受影響群體。

4. The company's profitability is susceptible to economic fluctuations. 公司的盈利能力對經濟波動非常敏感。

5. Children are susceptible to peer pressure. 孩子容易受到同儕

壓力的影響。

6. Her emotional state makes her susceptible to getting hurt. 她的感情狀態使她變得容易受傷。

Susceptible的同義詞及例句

1. Vulnerable（易受傷的）

He felt very vulnerable after the accident. 事故發生後，他感到非常脆弱。

2. Prone（傾向於）

She is prone to getting sunburned. 她容易被曬傷。

3. Sensitive（敏感的）

Her skin is very sensitive to certain cosmetics. 她的皮膚對某些化妝品非常敏感。

4. Open（易受的）

The system is open to security breaches. 這個系統容易受到安全漏洞的威脅。

5. Receptive（易接受的）

The audience was receptive to the speaker's ideas. 觀眾對演講者的想法很容易接受。

Intrepid vs Doughty
| 強悍的vs不屈不撓的

Intrepid勇猛的、無畏的

描述人或事物具有無所畏懼、勇敢面對困難或危險的特質。

1. The intrepid host, admired by netizens and supporters, publicly endorsing housing justice on their online livestream program has garnered widespread support from internet users. 那位強悍的主持人，在網友和粉絲的仰慕下，公開在他們的網路直播節目上支持居住正義，已經獲得了廣大網民的支持。

2. She is an intrepid explorer who travels to the most remote places on Earth. 她是一位無畏的探險家，前往地球上最偏遠的地方。

3. The intrepid firefighter rushed into the burning building to save lives. 那位勇敢的消防員衝進熊熊燃燒的建築物，拯救生命。

4. Despite the dangers, the intrepid journalist continued to report from war zones. 儘管危險重重，那位無畏的記者繼續在戰區報導。

Doughty和Intrepid都形容勇敢和無畏，但有些許不同之處

1. Doughty（堅毅的）：形容那些在面對困難、危險或挑戰

時表現出堅毅和不屈不撓的人。強調一種持久、堅定的勇氣，而不一定涵蓋到無所畏懼。

2. Intrepid（無畏的）：強調不會輕易感到害怕或退縮的性格特質。

Intrepid加強調無所畏懼，而Doughty強調堅韌和不屈不撓。因此，並不是完全相同的同義詞，但在某些上下文中可以互換使用，具體取決於語境。

Intrepid的同義英文單字

1. Fearless（無畏的）

   The fearless mountaineer climbed the treacherous peak without hesitation. 無畏的登山者毫不猶豫地攀登了危險的山峰。

2. Brave（勇敢的）

   The brave firefighter entered the burning building to rescue the trapped family. 勇敢的消防員進入熊熊燃燒的建築物，拯救被困的一家人。

3. Courageous（勇敢的）

   The courageous soldier faced the enemy with unwavering determination. 勇敢的士兵以堅定的決心面對敵人。

4. Valiant（英勇的）

   The valiant knight defended the kingdom against the dragon's onslaught. 英勇的騎士抵抗龍的猛攻，保衛了王國。

5. Daring（大膽的）

   Her daring plan led to a successful mission in hostile territory.

她大膽的計劃在敵對領土上帶來了一次成功的任務。

這些詞都可以用來描述那些無所畏懼、勇敢面對困難或危險的人或事物，具有相似的意義，可以根據具體的語境使用。

Doughty的同義字與例句

1. Indomitable（不屈不撓的）

   Her indomitable willpower helped her overcome great challenges. 她不屈不撓的意志力幫助她克服了巨大的挑戰。

Impeccable culinary skills
｜完美廚藝

Impeccable形容詞，完美無缺、無懈可擊的。

a man of impeccable character一個品格無可挑剔的人。

Impeccable應用及例句

1. Her impeccable taste in fashion always turns heads wherever she goes. 她對時尚的完美品味總是讓人眼前一亮。
2. The chef's impeccable culinary skills earned him a Michelin star. 這位廚師無可挑剔的烹飪技巧為他贏得了米其林星級評鑑。
3. The detective's impeccable attention to detail helped solve the complex case. 這名偵探對細節無懈可擊的關注幫助解決了這個複雜的案件。

與Impeccable相同或相近的單字

1. Flawless無瑕疵的、完美的
   Her performance in the play was flawless. 她在戲劇中的表現完美無瑕。
2. Perfect完美的
   The weather on our wedding day was absolutely perfect. 我們婚禮那天的天氣絕對完美。

3. Immaculate純潔的、無瑕疵的

The hotel room was immaculate, with no signs of dirt or dust. 酒店房間一塵不染，毫無塵土跡象。

4. Faultless無缺點的、完美的

Her knowledge of the subject is virtually faultless. 她對這個主題的知識幾乎是完美無缺的。

5. Exemplary典範的、可作爲榜樣的

His exemplary behavior earned him the respect of his peers. 他的典範行爲贏得了同儕的尊重。

6. Spotless一塵不染的、潔淨的

After hours of cleaning, the kitchen was spotless. 經過幾個小時的清潔，廚房一塵不染。

7. Unblemished無瑕的、無缺點的

Her record as a student is unblemished; she's never received a failing grade. 她作爲學生的記錄無瑕疵，她從未拿過不及格分數。

In cahoots | 沆瀣一氣

In cahoots合謀、狼狽爲奸、沆瀣一氣,指兩個或多個人或實體合作、密謀或勾結在一起,爲了實現某種共同的目標或祕密行動。

下文中,用來描述中國和俄羅斯似乎密謀合作或勾結在一起,共同對G7峰會的聲明做出憤怒回應:

China and Russia, seemingly in cahoots, have issued furious responses to the G7 summit declaration, asserting that this summit is brewing with anti-Russian and anti-Chinese sentiments.

中國和俄羅斯沆瀣一氣針對七大工業國G7峰會聲明做出憤怒回應,宣稱這場峰會是在醞釀反俄和反中的激動情緒。

與In cahoots相同概念的片語

1. In league with(與…同盟)

   The two companies were in league with each other to monopolize the market. 這兩家公司與彼此同盟,以壟斷市場。

2. In collusion with(與…串通一氣)

   The corrupt officials were in collusion with criminal organizations. 這些貪污官員與犯罪組織串通一氣。

3. Hand in glove with（與⋯密切合作）

The detective worked hand in glove with the informant to gather evidence. 這位偵探與線人密切合作，收集證據。

4. In partnership with（與⋯合夥）

The chef opened a restaurant in partnership with a renowned sommelier. 這位廚師與一位著名的品酒師合夥開了一家餐廳。

5. In cooperation with（與⋯合作）

The charity organization worked in cooperation with local volunteers to aid disaster victims. 這家慈善機構與當地志願者合作，協助災民。

以上這些片語都可表達人們或實體之間的密切合作或合謀關係。

Incorrigible｜無可救藥的

Incorrigible形容詞，無可救藥的、難以改變的、冥頑不靈的。當一個人或某種情況，通常指固執、難以改變或無法矯正的，尤其是指一個人的不良行為或壞習慣。暗示了一種不容易受到改善或修正的性質。

Incorrigible的例句

1. Sarah's lying habit was incorrigible; no matter how many times we talked to her, she continued to lie. 莎拉的說謊習慣是無法改變的；無論我們多次和她說她仍執意說謊。
2. The teacher found it difficult to deal with that group of students because they were incorrigible, refusing to accept instruction and disregarding rules. 老師發現難以應對那組學生，因為他們頑固不化，拒絕接受指導並不屑規定。

無可救藥的、冥頑不靈的單字

Irredeemable無可救藥的、Stubborn固執的、Intransigent不妥協的、Obstinate頑固的、Unyielding不屈服的、Intractable難以處理的、Unrepentant不悔改的、Obstinate頑固的、Resistant抵抗的、Unrepentant不悔改的。
這些詞彙都可用來形容某人或某事無可救藥的、冥頑不靈的或無法挽回的情況。

類似的字詞例句

1. Irredeemable（無可救藥的）

   His criminal record was so extensive that many considered him irredeemable. 他的犯罪紀錄如此多，許多人認為他無可挽回。

2. Stubborn（固執的）

   She can be quite stubborn when it comes to making decisions. 她在做決定時可以相當固執。

3. Intransigent（不妥協的）

   The union remained intransigent in their demands for higher wages. 工會在要求更高工資方面始終不妥協。

4. Obstinate（頑固的）

   His obstinate refusal to apologize created tension within the team. 他頑固地拒絕道歉導致團隊內部緊張。

5. Unyielding（不屈服的）

   The ancient oak tree stood unyielding in the face of strong winds. 古老的橡樹在強風面前屹立不倒。

6. Intractable（難以處理的）

   The intractable conflict between the two nations seemed to have no resolution. 兩國之間的難以處理衝突似乎沒有解決辦法。

7. Unrepentant（不悔改的）

   The criminal remained unrepentant, even after serving a long prison sentence. 即使在長時間監獄刑期結束後，這名罪犯仍不悔改。

8. Resistant（抵抗的）

The new material used in the construction is highly resistant to corrosion. 建築中使用的新材料對腐蝕有很高的抵抗力。

Immigrate vs Emigrate
有何差異？

Immigrate和Emigrate都涉及到人們從一個地方到另一個地方的移動，意思和用法不同。

Immigrate（移民、移居）

指的是人們進入新的國家或地區，通常是為了在那裡生活、工作或永久定居。強調的是「進入」新國家或地區的行為。

He immigrated to Canada for a better life. 他移民到加拿大，以追求更好的生活。

Emigrate（遷移或移出）

則指的是離開他們原來的國家或地區，通常是為了到達新的國家或地區。強調「離開原地」的行為。其他的同義字包括relocate、migrate。

She decided to emigrate from China to pursue her dreams in the United States. 她決定要從中國移出，去美國追求她的夢想。

其他移居或搬遷的英文單字

雖然這些都與移居或遷徙有關，但它們在特定情境中可能有些的差異，運用因情況而有所不同：

1. Migrate移居、遷徙。
2. Relocate搬遷、重新安置。

FancyEnglish 精湛英文

3. Resettle重新安頓、定居。

4. Move移動到新地方。

5. Depart離開，通常是永久性的離開。

6. Relocate移居、轉移。

7. Transplant移居、轉移（通常指在新地方建立新生活）。

Immigrate是指進入新國家或地區展開生活，而Emigrate是指離開原來的國家或地區。

Indecorous & Indecent

Indecorous和Indecent都有一定程度的相似性，因為它們都涉及到不適當或不得體的行為或言辭。

Indecorous

指不符合社會規範、禮儀或合適性的行為、言辭或舉止。側重於違反了通常被認為合適或得體的行為準則。

1. His indecorous behavior at the funeral shocked everyone in attendance. 他在葬禮上不得體的行為讓在場的人都感到震驚。
2. Using indecorous language in a professional setting can harm your reputation. 在職場環境中使用不得體的語言可能會損害您的聲譽。

Indecent

更加直接，意指淫穢、猥褻或不潔淨的，通常用來描述言談、行為或內容可能被認為是不適當或冒犯的情況。

1. The comedian's indecent jokes offended many members of the audience. 這位喜劇演員的猥褻笑話冒犯了許多觀眾。
2. Posting indecent images on social media platforms can result in legal consequences. 在社交媒體平台上發布猥褻圖片可能會帶來法律後果。

FancyEnglish 精湛英文

其他與這兩個詞有關的同義詞

1. Improper不適當或不得體的

   Wearing a swimsuit to a formal dinner is considered improper.
   穿泳衣參加正式晚宴被認爲是不適當的。

2. Unseemly不得體、不合適或不禮貌的

   His unseemly comments during the meeting offended many
   people. 他在會議期間的不得體評論冒犯了許多人。

3. Obscene淫穢、猥褻或令人不悅的內容

   The movie contained several obscene scenes that were not
   suitable for children. 這部電影包含幾個淫穢的場景，不適
   合兒童觀看。

4. Vulgar粗俗、低俗的。

   Her vulgar language and rude gestures shocked the audience.
   她的粗俗言談和粗魯手勢令觀眾感到震驚。

5. Tasteless沒有品味或不合適的

   The color combination in this painting is so tasteless; it lacks
   harmony. 這幅畫的色彩組合如此沒有品味，缺乏和諧
   感。

Ineffable | 難以言喻

Ineffable形容詞，難以形容、難以言喻的。描述那些無法用語言充分表達或形容的事物或感受。

Taiwanese people have an ineffable sense of warmth and fondness towards traveling to Japan. 台灣人對於日本旅遊有股不可言喻的親切感。

類似Ineffable的單字及例句

1. Inexpressible（形容詞）難以表達的

   The beauty of the sunset over the ocean was ineffable; no words could capture its true magnificence. 夕陽落在海洋上的美景是難以言喻的，無法用言語真正捕捉其壯麗之處。

2. Unutterable（形容詞）無法說出的

   The pain he felt upon hearing the news of his friend's passing was unutterable. 他聽到朋友去世的消息後所感受到的痛苦是無法言喻的。

3. Indescribable（形容詞）無法描述的

   The feeling of standing on top of the mountain and looking at the vast landscape below was indescribable. 站在山頂上，俯瞰著下方廣闊的風景，那種感覺是無法描述的。

Insolvent & inverted
| 破產潮

Insolvent是形容詞，名詞是Insolvency，指個體或組織無法支付其債務，處於財務困境或破產的狀態。其他與insolvent相近意思的詞語包括：Bankrupt、Debt-ridden、Inverted。

關於insolvent及insolvency的幾個例子

1. China's real estate and financial sectors are witnessing a wave of insolvencies, increasing the risk of a downward spiral in the Chinese economy. 中國的房地產和金融部門正見證一波破產潮，增加了中國經濟向下螺旋的風險。

2. The company declared bankruptcy after becoming insolvent. 這家公司因為財務狀況惡化而宣布破產。

3. When a business becomes insolvent, its assets are often liquidated to pay off creditors. 當一家企業陷入財務困境時，通常會出售資產以償還債權人。

在財務中使用Inverted時，意指負債或資產、收入不正常

1. The company's financial statements showed an inverted debt-to-equity ratio, which raised concerns among investors. 公司的財務報表顯示了「負債與股本比率倒掛」，引起了投資者的擔憂。

2. The company's revenue growth rate inverted this year, going

from positive to negative. 公司的收入增長率在今年倒轉，由正轉負。

3. Her financial situation is quite stable; she has an inverted debt-to-income ratio, with more income than debt. 她的財務狀況相當穩定；她的債務收入比率倒置，收入多於債務。

在這個句子中，Inverted指的是債務對資產或財富比率反轉或異常，這可能會對投資者造成擔憂。

Inundate｜抱怨「湧入」

Inundate動詞，淹沒、淹水，指某物被大量的液體覆蓋或充斥。Be inundated with指某物受到大量事物或訊息的淹沒，描述被壓倒性的數量或壓力。

As AI stock prices surged, customer orders inundated the system. Watching the stock prices soar, the fortunate investors couldn't help but smile from ear to ear.

隨著AI股價飆漲，客戶的訂單湧入系統。看著股價飆升，受惠的投資者情不自禁地樂開懷。（註：Smile from ear to ear 笑到合不攏嘴，樂開懷的意思。）

Inundate應用例子

1. My email inbox is constantly inundated with spam messages. 我的電子郵件收件匣總是被垃圾郵件淹沒。

2. After the announcement, the customer service hotline was inundated with calls from concerned customers. 公告後，客戶服務熱線被關切的客戶來電淹沒了。

其他與Inundate相似的單字片語

1. Overwhelm（壓倒性）

The news of the sudden loss of her loved one overwhelmed her with grief. 她突然失去親人的消息使她悲痛不已。

2. Overload（超載）

The electrical circuit couldn't handle the overload of power and short-circuited. 電路無法承受過多的電力，發生了短路。

3. Swamp（淹沒）

The heavy rain threatened to swamp the small village. 大雨威脅著淹沒這個小村莊。

4. Engulf（吞噬）

The massive wave engulfed the entire ship. 龐大的浪潮吞噬了整艘船。

Jocular | 幽默詼諧

Jocular形容詞，愛開玩笑的、幽默的、詼諧的。形容某人或某事有趣或愉快的性格或風格。

一起來閱讀某警局以詼諧影片引導青少年不要成為詐騙集團的棋子，如何運用單字Jocular：

A recent initiative by a police department features a jocular awareness video titled "Say No to Joining Criminal Organizations, Say No to Becoming a Scam Driver." In this engaging video, police officers take on acting roles, delivering both a captivating performance and humorous yet insightful narration. The message is clear: it warns young individuals against succumbing to short-term gains and becoming unwitting pawns of scam groups.

最近，一個警察局推出了jocular幽默宣導影片，標題為「拒絕加入犯罪組織、拒當詐欺車手」。在這個引人入勝的影片中，警察們扮演角色，既呈現出精彩的演出，又配以幽默而發人深思的旁白。影片傳達的訊息很明確：警告年輕人不要為了短期利益而沉迷，成為詐騙團的無知棋子。

來看看應用的例句

1. His jocular sense of humor always brightens up the office on a dull day. 他詼諧的幽默感總是能在無聊的日子裡為辦公室

帶來歡樂。

2. The comedian's jocular remarks had the entire audience laughing uncontrollably. 這位喜劇演員的詼諧言談讓整個觀眾笑得不可自制。

3. Despite the serious topic, he managed to maintain a jocular tone throughout his presentation. 儘管主題嚴肅，但他在整個演講中都保持著詼諧的口吻。

Jocular用來描述某人的輕鬆、愉快或幽默的態度，通常在輕鬆、幽默或愉快的情境下使用。

與Jocular相同或相近的字詞和片語

1. Humorous（形容詞）有趣或詼諧的
   His humorous anecdotes always entertain the guests at parties. 他幽默的趣聞軼事總是能娛樂到派對上的客人。

2. Witty（形容詞）機智和幽默的，指言詞上的智慧和幽默
   She's known for her witty remarks that keep everyone laughing. 她以機智的言詞而聞名，總是讓大家捧腹大笑。

3. Amusing（形容詞）有趣或可笑的
   The amusing antics of the playful kittens made everyone smile. 那些小貓咪有趣的惡作劇讓每個人都笑了。

4. Comical（形容詞）滑稽或可笑的，描述引發笑聲的事物
   The comedian's comical impersonations of famous celebrities were a hit. 這位喜劇演員對著名人的滑稽模仿大受歡迎。

5. Lighthearted（形容詞）輕鬆愉快的，不受負面情緒影響的

They had a lighthearted conversation over dinner, sharing jokes and stories. 他們在晚餐時進行了一場輕鬆愉快的對話，分享笑話和故事。

Keep a low profile.
| 保持低調

保持低調的短文及例句

1. The media reported that the president's transit in the United States always deliberately kept a low profile to avoid unnecessary influence. 媒體報導總統過境美國時刻意保持低調，避免引發不必要的影響。

2. I advise you to keep a low profile during the investigation to avoid drawing unnecessary attention. 我建議你在調查期間保持低調，以避免引起不必要的注意。

3. After the controversy, the celebrity decided to keep a low profile and stay out of the public eye for a while. 在爭議之後，這位名人決定保持低調，暫時遠離公眾視線。

4. In a competitive industry, it's often wise for businesses to keep a low profile until they are ready to launch their new product. 在競爭激烈的行業中，企業通常會在準備好推出新產品之前保持低調。

低調奢華Low-key luxury、低調時尚Understated fashion、低調風格 Low-key style等英文例句

1. She prefers a low-key luxury lifestyle, with elegant but not overly flashy possessions. 她喜歡低調奢華的生活方式，擁有優雅但不過於炫耀的物品。

2. His understated fashion sense consists of classic pieces that never go out of style. 他低調的時尚品味包括永不過時的經典單品。

3. The party had a low-key style, with simple decorations and a relaxed atmosphere. 派對風格低調，裝飾簡單，氣氛輕鬆。

Laggy | My laptop is laggy.
我的筆電很「卡」

Laggy形容詞，描述事物運行緩慢的或反應遲緩的。例如：My smartphone is so laggy that it takes forever to open any app. 我的智慧型手機反應如此緩慢以至於打開任何應用程式都要花費很長時間。My laptop is laggy我的筆電很卡。

Lag是名詞也是動詞，名詞使用時，它表示延遲或滯後。The lag in the video stream made it difficult to follow the game. 串流的延遲使得難以跟上比賽進度。

當Lag作為動詞，它表示滯後或延遲。The computer started to lag after opening multiple applications simultaneously.在同時打開多個應用程式後，電腦開始出現滯後現象。

和**Laggy**同義的英文單字與例句

1. Sluggish

   The internet connection in the remote area is often sluggish, making it difficult to stream videos. 偏遠地區的網絡連接經常很遲緩，使得難以流視頻。

2. Delayed

   The train service is currently delayed due to technical issues. 目前列車服務因技術問題而延誤。

3. Unresponsive

My smartphone became unresponsive after the software update, and I had to restart it. 軟體更新後，我的智慧型手機變得不靈敏，不得不重新啟動它。

Laggy傾向形容技術或設備的性能問題運行緩慢或反應遲緩。

形容人的遲到、會延、愚鈍或反應遲緩的則是使用 tardy或obtuse

1. Tardy遲到或延誤，表示某人或某事的行動或到達時間晚於預期或規定的時間。

   He was tardy for the meeting. 他會議遲到了。

2. Obtuse遲鈍或愚鈍，形容理解力、反應或思維方式不夠靈活。

   His obtuse response showed he didn't grasp the concept. 他遲鈍的回答顯示他沒有理解這個概念。

Lethargy | 無力感

Lethargy名詞，指一種身體或精神上的無力感，通常伴隨著缺乏動力或興趣。

來看看以下的幾個例子

1. After a long week of work and stress, he was overcome by lethargy and spent the entire weekend on the couch. 經過一個繁忙的工作週，他感到無力，整個週末都窩在沙發上。

2. The sizzling hot and humid weather often leads to a sense of lethargy, making it difficult to focus on tasks. 炎熱潮濕的天氣常常會導致無力感，使人難以集中注意力完成任務。

3. Her lethargy was evident in her lack of enthusiasm during the meeting, and it was clear she needed a break. 她在會議中表現出的無力感使人一目了然，顯然她需要休息一下。

與Lethargy相近同義的單字，以及說明例句

1. Apathy冷漠：A lack of interest, enthusiasm, or concern.
   His apathy towards the environmental issues was evident when he refused to participate in the clean-up effort. 他對環境問題的冷漠在他拒絕參加清潔工作時表露無遺。

2. Lassitude疲倦：A state of physical or mental weariness, often characterized by lack of energy.

The long hike left her in a state of lassitude, and she needed a rest. 長途徒步使她感到疲倦不堪，她需要休息。

3. Torpor（名詞）遲鈍：A state of physical or mental inactivity, sluggishness, or dormancy.

The extreme heat induced a sense of torpor in the afternoon, causing everyone to feel sluggish. 極端的熱天氣使人下午感到遲鈍，每個人都感到沉悶不安。

4. Listlessness無精打采：A lack of interest or energy, often resulting in a sense of being without purpose.

His listlessness in class was a clear sign that he wasn't engaged in the subject. 他在課堂上的無精打采顯示出他對這門學科不感興趣。

Lie flat、Slack off、Veg out | 躺平、擺爛、耍廢

Lie flat躺平

意味著平躺或仰臥。同義詞包括lie down和recline。

After a long day at work, I like to lie flat on the couch and relax. 工作了一整天後，我喜歡躺平在沙發上放鬆。

「躺平文化」Lie flat culture：

Young people are increasingly choosing an attitude of lying flat, where they have no desires and opt to veg out rather than conforming to societal expectations and striving. 年輕人越來越傾向於選擇一種「躺平」的態度，他們不再有願望，選擇放鬆而不是遵循社會期望和努力奮鬥。

Slack off擺爛、偷懶

同義詞包括procrastinate和be lazy。

You shouldn't slack off when there's still work to be done. 還有工作要做的時候，你不應該偷懶。

Veg out耍廢、放鬆

指的是過度放鬆或無所作為，包括長時間地坐著或躺著，不做有意義的事情。同義詞是laze around或idle away。

On weekends, I like to veg out in front of the TV and watch movies. 週末時，我喜歡在電視前耍廢，看電影。

Mellifluous │ 悅耳動聽

Mellifluous是形容詞，形容聲音或音樂時的柔和、流暢、悅耳。日前有報導指出某玉女歌手之女不但遺傳了良好基因，而且還歌聲悅耳，我們來看一下怎麼把這個單字（悅耳的Mellifluous）套用在文章之中使用：

In the 1980s, the mellifluous female singer passed down her good genes to her daughter. Not only did she inherit her mother's graceful beauty, but she also possessed a mellifluous voice and a remarkable singing talent. She even auditioned for talent shows, showcasing her enchanting voice on a grand stage.

80年代甜美的玉女歌手，的女兒遺傳到母親的好基因，不但長得亭亭玉立，歌聲悅耳還有一副好歌喉，曾參加選秀節目海選。

Mellifluous例子的應用

1. Her mellifluous voice filled the concert hall with enchanting melodies. 她的甜美聲音充滿了音樂廳，奏出迷人的旋律。

2. The mellifluous sound of the flowing river was incredibly soothing. 那條流水的悅耳聲音非常舒緩。

3. The mellifluous notes of the piano captured the hearts of the audience. 鋼琴優美的音符俘虜了觀眾的心靈。

描述聲音或音樂時，和**Mellifluous** 相似的詞

1. Euphonious（和聲的，悅耳的，和諧的）：形容聲音悅耳動聽。

   The euphonious melodies of the violin charmed the audience. 小提琴的和諧旋律迷住了觀眾。

2. Melodious（旋律美妙的，悅耳的）：形容音樂或聲音充滿旋律和音調的美感。

   The melodious singing of the birds signaled the arrival of spring. 鳥兒的美妙歌聲預示著春天的到來。

3. Harmonious（和諧的，協調的，和睦的）：強調聲音或音樂中各個部分和諧統一的特性。

   The harmonious blend of instruments created a captivating symphony. 各樂器的和諧統一創造出迷人的交響樂。

Mercurial | 變化多端

Mercurial形容詞，形容人或事物變化多端、反應快速、情緒多變、或不穩定的特質。用來描述個人行為或情感的不穩定性。

來看一段醫學的報導有關淋巴癌號成為「變化多端」的腫瘤，看看將如何將Mercurial在應用在文章內：

In Taiwan, approximately 3,000 new cases of lymphoma are diagnosed each year. Many celebrities and entrepreneurs have also been affected by lymphoma. Lymphoma falls under the category of cancers with extremely high diagnostic and treatment complexities. It can manifest in various organs and tissues within the body, often leading to confusion with other diseases. Careful discrimination in diagnosis is essential, earning it the nickname the mercurial tumor.

在台灣，每年約有約3,000例淋巴癌的新病例被診斷出來。許多名人和企業家也受到淋巴癌的影響。淋巴癌屬於診斷和治療極其複雜的癌症之一。它可以在身體的各個器官和組織中表現出來，常常容易與其他疾病混淆。在診斷時需要非常謹慎的鑑別，因此被稱為「多變的腫瘤」。

Mercurial的例句及應用

1. Her mercurial personality made it difficult to predict how she would react to different situations. 她多變的個性讓人難以

預測她對不同情況的反應。

2. The stock market can be quite mercurial, with prices fluctuating rapidly. 股市可能變動迅速，價格波動大。

3. His mercurial moods often left his friends feeling unsure about how to approach him. 他多變的情緒經常讓朋友們感到不確定應該如何接近他。

Mercurial的同義詞詞彙以及例句

1. Unpredictable（不可預測的）：指難以預測或變化多端的情況。

   Her moods are as unpredictable as the weather. 她的情緒變化如同天氣一般難以預測。

2. Fickle（善變的）：形容人或情況容易變化，不穩定。

   The stock market can be quite fickle, with prices fluctuating rapidly. 股市可能相當善變，價格波動迅速。

3. Capricious（反覆無常的）：形容某人或某事隨心所欲地變化。

   The capricious nature of the wind made sailing a challenge. 風的反覆無常性使得航行變得具有挑戰性。

4. Volatile（不穩定的）：描述容易快速變化或爆發的狀態。

   The volatile chemicals required careful handling. 這些不穩定的化學品需要小心處理。

5. Erratic（不規則的）：指的是行為或運動缺乏規律性。

   His erratic driving made other motorists nervous. 他不規則的駕駛讓其他駕駛者感到緊張。

Misogyny｜厭女

「厭女症」Misogyny也就是Dislike of, contempt for, or ingrained prejudice against women.來看一下厭女症的英文描述：

Misogyny is a complex issue with possible reasons including cultural and historical factors, such as the long-standing belief in male superiority, which may have been passed down through generations. Cultural, religious, traditional, online media and power structures can all play a role in shaping people's perceptions of gender roles. To combat misogyny, a range of educational, promotional, and policy measures are needed to establish a more equal and inclusive society. This requires long-term efforts, from the individual level to institutional change.

厭女症發酵是複雜的問題，牽涉文化和歷史因素，像是長期以來，男性被認為優越於女性，這種觀念可能被傳承下來。文化、宗教、傳統、網路媒體及權利結構等因素都有可能以塑造人們對性別角色的看法。要對抗厭女症，需要一系列教育、宣傳和政策措施，建立更平等和包容的社會。這需要長期的努力，從個人層面到制度層面的改變。

來看看「厭女症」的應用

1. Misogyny is a harmful attitude that promotes discrimination against women. 厭女症是一種有害的態度，促使對女性的

歧視。

2. It's crucial to address misogyny in society to achieve gender equality. 在社會中解決厭女情結是實現性別平等的重要關鍵。

3. Some forms of online harassment are driven by misogyny, targeting women with hate speech. 一些形式的網絡騷擾是由厭女情結驅使的，針對女性使用仇恨言論。

4. Misogyny perpetuates harmful stereotypes about women, limiting their opportunities. 厭女情結延續了對女性的有害刻板印象，限制了她們的機會。

Mundane | 平凡的例行公事

Do you want to get way from another mundane routines of daily life?

Just another ordinary day. 、Just another mundane day. 平凡的一天Have an extraordinary day. 、Have a fantastic day.有個特別的一天

來看看例子

1. His job required him to tackle both mundane tasks and complex challenges, making his work varied and interesting. 他的工作要求他既要應對平凡的任務，又要應對複雜的挑戰，使得他的工作多變又有趣。

2. She found solace in the beauty of painting, away from the mundane routines of daily life. 她在繪畫之美中找到了慰藉，遠離了日常生活的平凡。

Nugatory | 無關緊要

Nugatory形容詞，無關緊要、不重要或無價值的事物或行為。

來看一下Nugatory在英文一篇財經評級短文中的運用情形：
Moody's, the American financial institution, downgraded the United States' credit rating from AAA to AA+; however, financial experts consider this move nugatory, as concerns about the country's fiscal situation over the next three years were already anticipated.
穆迪公司，美國的金融機構，將美國的信用評級從AAA降級為AA+；然而，金融專家認為這個舉動無關緊要，因為對未來三年內該國財政狀況的擔憂已被預期。

其他例句應用

1. His nugatory excuses for being late to work were no longer accepted by his boss. 他對於遲到上班的無關緊要藉口已不再被老闆接受。

2. The committee found the proposed changes to be nugatory and decided to maintain the current policy. 委員會認為所提出的變更是無關緊要的，決定保持現行政策。

3. Spending hours arguing about the color of the office carpet seemed nugatory in the grand scheme of things. 花了數小時

爭論辦公室地毯的顏色，在整體規劃中似乎毫無價值。

Nugatory相近意思的單字以及例句

1. Insignificant（微不足道的）

   The tiny scratch on the car was insignificant. 車上的微小刮痕毫無意義。

2. Trivial（瑣碎的）

   His trivial complaints annoyed everyone. 他的瑣碎抱怨讓每個人都感到煩惱。

3. Paltry（微不足道的）

   The paltry sum of money he offered was insulting. 他提供的微不足道的金額是侮辱性的。

4. Meaningless（毫無意義的）

   The conversation was so meaningless that I lost interest. 這個對話太毫無意義，我失去了興趣。

Obdurate
頑強抵抗／頑固症頭

Obdurate形容詞，描述人或事物固執、不肯改變、不易感化的性格或態度。Bleach can effectively tackle obdurate mold. 漂白水可以有效處理頑固的霉。

頑固憂鬱症怎麼說？來看一下以下的短文：

One of the personality traits often displayed by people with obdurate depression is overcontrol or over repression. In other words, the symptoms of the patients did not improve, not because they were not motivated enough or not working hard enough; on the contrary, it may be because they worked too hard. 頑固性憂鬱症患者經常表現出的人格特徵之一是過度控製或過度壓抑。換句話說，患者的症狀沒有改善，並不是因爲他們動力不夠，或者不夠努力；而是因爲他們的積極性不夠。相反，可能是因爲他們太努力了。

Obdurate的例句應用

1. She was so obdurate in her refusal to compromise that the negotiation stalled. 她在拒絕妥協方面如此固執，以至於談判陷入停滯。

2. Despite numerous attempts to convince him, his obdurate attitude remained unchanged. 儘管多次嘗試說服他，但他

的固執態度仍然不變。

3. The obdurate resistance of the old tree to disease and harsh weather was truly remarkable. 這棵老樹對疾病和惡劣天氣的頑強抵抗力真是令人驚訝的。

與Obdurate相似的英文同義字和例句

1. Obstinate（堅定的／頑固的）

The President's overseas visit signifies that our determination to step onto the world stage will only grow more obstinate, unwavering. 總統的海外訪問象徵著我們踏上世界舞台的決心將變得越來越頑固，堅定不移。

2. Stubborn（固執的）表示人不容易改變他們的想法或立場

Despite numerous attempts to persuade him, John remained stubborn about his decision to quit the job. 儘管多次嘗試說服他，約翰對於辭職的決定仍然固執不變。

3. Inflexible（不靈活的）指人事物不容易適應新的情況或變化

The company's inflexible policies made it difficult for employees to request time off. 公司的不靈活政策讓員工難以請假。

4. Resolute（堅決的）有堅定的意志，不會輕易妥協

She remained resolute in her pursuit of justice, despite facing many challenges. 儘管面臨許多挑戰，她在追求正義方面保持著堅定的意志。

5. Unyielding（強硬的／不屈服的）人或事物不會屈服或讓步

The unyielding mountain terrain posed a significant challenge to the hikers. 強硬的山地地形對徒步旅行者構成了重大挑戰。

6. Intransigent（不妥協的）拒絕變通或妥協

The intransigent negotiators could not reach a compromise. 不妥協的談判代表無法達成妥協。

7. intractable（頑固的／難以控制）

The defendant's personality is incredibly intractable, completely denying all the evidence presented by the prosecutor. 這個被告的個性十分頑固對於檢察官所提出的所有證據完全否認。

這些詞彙都可以用來描述那些固執、不容易改變或不易感化的性格或態度。希望這些例子能幫助你更好地理解它們的用法和意義。

Opportunistic｜投機取巧

「投機取巧」也是中文說的滑頭滑腦，態度不一致是會招致非議的，這則新聞就是例子：

French President Macron's opportunistic policies, both domestically and internationally, have led the public to view him as a cunning political figure who capitalizes on shifting circumstances.

法國總統馬克宏的機會主義政策，無論在國內還是國際上，都讓公眾認為他是一位狡猾的政治人物，善於利用不斷變化的情勢。（註Capitalize on充分、善加利用，指善用機會或情勢以獲得利益或成功。在上述中，指的是馬克宏利用政策中的機會或變化來獲得政治利益。）

「投機取巧」或類似的概念的單字

1. 「投機取巧」的英文可以表達為cut corners或take shortcuts。

   Cut corners：He always tries to take corners to save time, but it's not always the safest option. 他總是試圖走彎路以節省時間，但這並不總是最安全的選擇。

   Take shortcuts：She often takes shortcuts in her work, which can lead to mistakes. 她在工作中經常走捷徑，這可能導致錯誤。

2. opportunistic趁機而為，為了自己的好處，試圖從機會中

獲益，而不一定遵守嚴格的規則或道德標準。

She has an opportunistic nature, always looking for ways to benefit from any situation. 她投機取巧的本領，總是尋找從任何情況中獲利的方法。

3. Unscrupulous為了達到個人目的，無道德或不擇手段的行為。

His unscrupulous business practices eventually result in legal trouble. 他不道德的商業行為最終導致了法律麻煩。

4. Cutthroat指競爭激烈且不擇手段，可能包括投機取巧。

5. Shrewd聰明和精明，有時可以指某人能夠巧妙地利用機會。

His shrewd investments made him a wealthy man. 他精明的投資使他成為了一個富有的人。

6. Scheming策劃或陰謀，形容不誠實或投機行為。

In the world of corporate competition, cutthroat scheming is unfortunately common. 在企業競爭的世界中，充斥著投機取巧的競爭行為。

He rose to power through a combination of cutthroat scheming and ruthless tactics. 他通過投機取巧的策略和無情的手段崛起至權力之巔。

以上的句子分別強調了各自詞語或片語的不同用法，都涉及了投機，或是對機會和效率的利用。

Oblivious | 漠不關心

Oblivious形容詞，形容某人對於周圍情況或事物毫無察覺或不知情。通常在以下情境下使用：
1. 描述某人對周圍環境的漠不關心或不關心。
2. 形容某人對於某事的無知或不在意。

如何將Oblivious運用在關於夏威夷大火災難後，當局漠不關心的消息：

The death toll from the Hawaii wildfire has risen to 106, and residents criticize the authorities for being oblivious to the plight of those fighting for survival. They are spontaneously gathering supplies and setting up rescue centers, coming together to be each other's rescuers.

夏威夷山火罹難數增至106人，居民批當局對絕地逢生的居民漠不關心，他們正自發募集物資、搭建救援中心，齊心協力成為彼此的救難人員。

再來看一下例句的應用

1. He was so lost in thought that he was oblivious to the people passing by him. 他陷入了沉思，以至於對於路過他的人毫不在意。
2. She seemed oblivious to the fact that her phone was ringing loudly during the meeting. 她似乎對於會議期間她的手機大

聲響起這個事實毫不在意。

3. The child was playing so happily that he was oblivious to the time passing. 這個孩子玩得如此開心，以至於對於時間的流逝毫不在意。

4. She was so engrossed in her book that she was oblivious to the loud noise outside. 她太沉浸於書中，以至於對外面的噪音完全不知情。

Oblivious的同義詞

1. Unaware不知道，未察覺的

   He was unaware of the changes happening around him. 他對周圍的變化一無所知。

2. Ignorant無知的，不了解的

   She remained ignorant of the fact that the meeting had been canceled. 她仍然不知道會議已經取消了。

3. Clueless毫無頭緒的，不知所措的

   He looked completely clueless when asked about the topic. 當問及該話題時，他顯得完全不知所措。

4. Unconscious無意識的，未察覺的

   She remained unconscious of the danger lurking nearby. 她對附近潛在的危險毫無察覺。

Opulent | 富饒／富裕

Opulent形容詞，非常富裕、豐富或奢華的。
通常在以下情境使用：
1. 形容富有或華麗的生活方式、建築物、裝飾等。
2. 形容某地區或國家的繁榮和富裕程度。
3. 形容豐富多彩的文化、藝術或風景。

來看看以下應用的例句

1. The opulent mansion featured marble floors, crystal chandeliers, and gold-plated fixtures. 這座豪華的大宅擁有大理石地板、水晶吊燈和鍍金裝置。
2. The opulent display of jewelry in the store's window left everyone in awe. 商店櫥窗中豐富的珠寶陳列讓每個人都感到驚嘆。
3. The opulent history of the city could be seen in its grand cathedrals and historic palaces. 這座城市豐富的歷史可以從它的宏偉大教堂和歷史宮殿中看出來。

Opulent的同義詞

1. Wealthy富有，擁有豐裕的
   The wealthy businessman owned multiple luxury cars. 這位富有的商人擁有多輛豪華汽車。
2. Affluent擁有豐富資源或財富的，經濟充裕的

The neighborhood was known for its affluent residents and elegant homes. 這個社區以富裕的居民和優雅的住宅而聞名。

3. Prosperous經濟繁榮的

The city experienced a period of prosperous growth in the 20th century. 這個城市在20世紀經歷了一段繁榮增長時期。

4. Lavish奢華和慷慨，通常指花費大量金錢

The wedding reception was a lavish affair with exquisite decorations and gourmet cuisine. 婚禮接待非常奢華，有精美的裝飾和美食。

5. Sumptuous華麗和豐盛，特別指食物或住宿的奢侈

The sumptuous banquet featured a variety of gourmet dishes. 這場豐盛的宴會提供了各種美食。

Splendid和Opulent有一些相似之處，但意思略有不同

Splendid是形容詞，通形容事物非常出色、壯觀、華麗、令人印象深刻或美麗。Opulent也是形容詞，形容富裕、豐裕、奢華的事物，強調財富和資源豐富。

The palace was opulent with its gold decorations and marble floors, and the royal ball held there was truly splendid. 這座宮殿由於其金裝飾和大理石地板而極其奢華，皇家舞會在那裡舉行，真的非常壯觀。

在這個例子中，Opulent描述宮殿的豐裕和奢華，而splendid描述了皇家舞會的壯觀和美麗。儘管它們有關聯，但意義略有不同。

Pale in comparison
| 黯然失色

也可以用Pale by comparison表示，意指相較之下相形見絀或是黯然失色，不如其他事物或情況引人注目或重要。

來看一篇有關在房市景氣短文的應用：

The real estate expert believes that a major housing market crash is looming, and he also suggests that compared to the impending crisis in 2023, the 2008 crisis will pale in comparison. In his tweet, he wrote, 2008 was a global financial crisis, whereas 2023 will make the 2008 global financial crisis pale in comparison.

這位房地產專家相信一場重大的房市崩盤即將來臨，並且他也建議，與即將到來的2023年危機相比，2008年的危機將相形見絀。在他的推文中，他寫到：「2008年是一場全球金融危機，而2023年將使2008年的全球金融危機相形見絀。

Pale in comparison 的例句及應用

1. His accomplishments pale in comparison to those of his older brother. 他的成就與他的哥哥相比顯得黯然失色。

2. The new smartphone's features make the old one pale in comparison. 新手機的功能使得舊的手機相形見絀。

3. The local park's playground is nice, but it pales in comparison

to the massive amusement park nearby. 這個地方公園的遊樂場很不錯，但與附近的大型遊樂園相比則相形見絀。

這些例句中都表現出一個事物或情況相對於另一個而言不足或不重要的概念。

Fall short of和Pale in comparison在某些情境可以互換使用

都表示某物相對於另一物不足或遜色，以下是應用的用法：
Fall short of（相對不足）His efforts fell short of his colleague's outstanding performance. 他的努力相對不足，無法與同事出色的表現相媲美。

Parched | 極度乾燥

Parched形容詞，描述物體或人口渴且極度乾燥的狀態。通常用來描述乾旱的地區、渴望飲水的人，或其他缺水的情況。

看一下應用的例句

1. The desert was so hot and dry that the ground appeared parched, with no sign of water for miles. 沙漠太炎熱且極度乾燥，地面看起來乾癟，數英里內都看不到水源。

2. After a long hike in the sun, they were parched and desperately in need of a cold drink. 經過長時間的陽光下遠足後，他們口渴極了，迫切需要一杯冰涼的飲料。

3. The prolonged drought left the farmland parched and unproductive, causing hardship for the farmers. 長時間的乾旱使農田變得乾枯，作物無法生長，對農民造成了困難。

和Parched相似的單字和詞語

1. Dehydrated（脫水）：失去水分，通常指身體或物體因缺乏水分而變得乾燥。
   After the long hike, he felt dehydrated and needed to drink water. 長時間的遠足後，他感到脫水，需要喝水。

2. Dry（乾燥）：缺乏濕氣或水分的狀態，使物體變得乾燥。

The dry climate in the desert makes the soil parched and infertile. 沙漠中的乾燥氣候使土壤變得乾枯且貧瘠。

3. Arid（乾旱）：指地區缺乏降雨或水源，導致乾旱和乾燥。

The arid region rarely sees rain, leaving the land parched and barren. 這個乾旱地區很少下雨，土地變得乾燥而荒蕪。

4. Thirsty（口渴）：渴望水分的感覺，通常指身體需要水來解渴。

After a strenuous workout, she was so thirsty that she drank a whole bottle of water. 經過一次激烈的運動後，她口渴極了，喝了一整瓶水。

這些詞彙都與Parched有類似的意思，都涉及到缺乏水分的或乾燥的狀態，但有時具有不同的用法和強調。

Patronize | 支持或贊助

照顧、光顧、支持及贊助的意思。

例句

1. The government decided to patronize the development of renewable energy sources to combat climate change.
   政府決定支持可再生能源的發展，以對抗氣候變化。這邊就是支持或鼓勵的意思。

2. The wealthy businessman liked to patronize the arts, often attending gallery openings and buying valuable paintings.
   這位富有的商人喜歡支持藝術，經常參加畫廊開幕式並購買有價值的畫作。

3. She didn't want to patronize the new restaurant because she had heard mixed reviews about it.
   她不想光顧那家新餐廳，因為她聽說有關它的評價褒貶不一。

常用特殊的用法：Don't patronize me.

「不要把我當小孩」或「不要呼嚨我」也可以用其他的方式表示：

1. Don't treat me like a child. 不要把我當成小孩子。
2. Don't talk down to me. 不要對我居高臨下。
3. Don't condescend to me. 不要對我傲慢。

4. I don't need your patronizing attitude.我不需要你的高姿態。

以下例句都有「呼嚨、輕視」的意思

1. It's important not to patronize children but rather engage them in meaningful conversations. 重要的是不要對待輕視孩子，而是與他們進行有意義的對話。

2. Don't patronize me with your so-called advice; I know what I am doing. 我不要你的高傲的建議；我知道我在做什麼。

3. He always patronizes his younger brother, treating him like a child. 他總是「呼嚨」對待他的弟弟，像對待小孩一樣。

4. It is frustrating when people patronize you just because you are new to the team. 當人們只因為你是新手就輕視你，這真是令人沮喪。

Peccadillo｜瑕不掩瑜

Peccadillo is a noun that describes a minor, small mistake, fault, or defect. This word is typically used to characterize insignificant, harmless errors or behaviors that usually do not result in serious consequences or punishment. It is sometimes also used to refer to minor moral lapses but still of a relatively mild nature.

是名詞，意思是輕微的過失、小錯誤、微罪或小瑕疵，通常是無關緊要的瑕疵，或是「瑕不掩瑜」的感受。

使用情境如下：

1. 在談論個人行為或行為中的小錯誤時。
2. 在評論某事物或情況中的小缺陷或不完美之處時。
3. 用於輕鬆或非正式的對話中，以指出輕微的錯誤或缺點。

當作瑕不掩時，運用在時機及使用方法可以這樣說：

Despite a series of peccadillos occurring during this overseas trip, the politician remained steadfast in pursuing and successfully completing the scheduled itinerary and tasks. It can be said that these minor flaws did not overshadow his achievements, making him worthy of admiration and encouragement.

儘管在此次海外參訪期間發生了一連串小錯誤，這位政治家仍然堅定地追求並成功完成了預定的行程和任務。可以說，這些小瑕疵並未掩蓋他的成就，使他值得受到讚賞和鼓勵。

應用的例句示範

1. His constant tardiness is just a peccadillo, nothing to be too concerned about. 他經常性的遲到只是小錯誤，不值得太擔心。

2. While the movie had its flaws, they were merely peccadillos in an otherwise enjoyable experience. 雖然這部電影有些缺點，但仍讓人覺得瑕不掩瑜。

3. Sarah forgave John for his peccadilloes and chose to focus on their strong emotional connection. 莎拉原諒了約翰的小錯誤，選擇專注於他們之間強烈的情感聯繫。

4. Her occasional temper tantrums are just peccadillos; they don't overshadow her many admirable qualities. 她偶爾的脾氣暴躁只是小錯誤，並不掩蓋她許多令人欽佩的品質。

Peccadillo的同義詞及範例

1. Faux pas（失言、失態）社交上的失言或失態

   She made a faux pas by bringing up their recent breakup at the dinner party. 她在晚宴上談到了他們最近的分手，犯了個失態。（註：Faux pas是法語詞彙，作名詞使用，指社交或禮儀上的失誤、疏忽或不得體的行為。描述在特定社交或文化情境下不得體或令人尷尬的舉止。）

2. Indiscretion（不慎、輕率）缺乏謹慎或輕率行為

   His indiscretion in sharing confidential information cost him his job. 他不慎洩露機密資訊，付出了失去工作的代價。

3. Minor transgression（小過失、輕微罪行）輕微的違法行為

Speeding is a minor transgression, but it can lead to accidents.
超速是一個小過失，但可能導致事故。

4. Lapse（失誤、疏忽）一時的錯誤或疏忽

Her lapse in judgment led to financial problems. 她判斷不慎，導致了財務困難。

5. Peccancy（罪過、不道德）不道德或有罪的行為

The peccancy of his actions was clear to everyone. 他的行為的罪惡性對每個人都是明顯的。（註：Peccancy是少見的英語詞彙，描述不道德、不合法或有罪的過錯。替代詞是Wrongdoing不端行為或Sinfulness有罪性。）

這些詞語都可以用來描述小的、不重要的錯誤或罪行，通常是在道德或社交上的。

Polarize vs Poles asunder
兩極化vs極端分裂

Polarization「兩極化」和Poles asunder「極端分開」不是相同的意思，但它們都與對立或極端相關。

Polarization兩極化

通常指的是社會、政治或文化上的分裂，其中人們傾向於支持極端立場，而忽視中間立場或妥協。兩極化意味著人們分為兩個極端的陣營，之間的共識變得困難。

1. The controversial debate over gun control has polarized the nation, with people taking extreme positions on both sides. 關於槍支管制的爭議性辯論已經使整個國家極度分裂，人們在立場上採取了兩個極端立場。

2. Social media can sometimes polarize public opinion by amplifying extreme viewpoints and suppressing moderate voices. 社交媒體有時會極化公眾意見，放大極端觀點，壓制溫和聲音。

3. The election results revealed a deeply polarized electorate, highlighting the divide within the country. 選舉結果顯示出選民深刻的分歧，凸顯了國家內部的分裂。

Poles Asunder極端分開

這個短語比較少見，但它傳達了事物被分開到極端的程度。

Poles在這裡指的是極端或對立的位置，而asunder表示被分開或撕裂。因此poles asunder意味著事物被分開到極端的程度，通常伴隨著很大的距離或差異。

1. The earthquake tore the building's support beams apart, splitting them like poles asunder. 地震將建築物的支撐樑徹底撕裂，就像將它們撕成兩半一樣。

2. Their disagreement on the project's direction drove a wedge between the two partners, tearing their business partnership poles asunder. 他們在項目方向上的意見分歧在兩位合夥人之間製造了分歧，撕裂了他們的商業夥伴關係。

3. The sudden revelation of his double life shattered their marriage, ripping their trust poles asunder. 他的雙重生活突然曝光，粉碎了他們的婚姻，撕裂了他們的信任。

雖然這兩個詞都與極端或對立有關，但它們的語境和用法有所不同。「兩極化」更常用，用於描述社會和政治現象，而poles asunder用於形容事物之間的極端分離。

Peremptory vs Preemptory

這兩個英文單字，看似相近，但意義不同。

Peremptory（形容詞）

強硬、霸道、專斷、不容反駁的，通常帶有命令性質；同義詞有authoritative、dictatorial、imperative、commanding、arbitrary、bossy。

1. The Health Authority's epidemic control center has taken peremptory measures, swiftly upgrading border controls, significantly strengthening quarantine, and promptly amending laws to address the needs of epidemic containment. 衛生署疫情指揮中心已經採取了「斷然措施」，迅速升級邊境管制，大幅強化檢疫，並且快速修改法律以應對疫情擴散的需要。

2. Parents, with their peremptory approach, demand their children to study or restrict their entertainment, leading to the opposite result often. 父母以他們的專斷方式要求孩子讀書或限制他們的娛樂，往往導致相反的結果。

Preemptory（形容詞）

先發制人、搶占先機或預先占據某種地位的情況，同義詞有preemptive、anticipatory、proactive。

1. Chairman's preemptory decision to cancel the meeting surprised everyone. 主席先發制人取消會議的決定讓每個人都感到驚訝。
2. The United States has implemented a preemptive measure by imposing restrictions on the export of advanced semiconductor manufacturing processes and AI technology to China. 美國已採取預防性措施，對出口先進半導體製程和AI技術至中國實施限制。

Prescient｜預知未來

1. Prescient有預知未來的能力或洞察力
2. With foresight有預見性或有提前考慮未來的能力
3. Auspicious好兆頭或幸運的
4. A prophetic token一個預言性的象徵或預兆

Japanese female manga artist Long Shuliang（たつき守）claims that her prescient savant ability is comparable to that of an Indian child prodigy. In 1999, she published the comic The Future I See, which included 15 of her prophetic dreams.
日本女性漫畫家龍樹良（たつき守）聲稱她的預知天賦可媲美印度的童奇才。1999年她出版了漫畫《我所見的未來》，其中包含了她15個先知性的夢境。

其他單字的例句應用

1. Prescient（預知）

   The author's prescient predictions about technology in the 21st century amazed readers. 這位作者對21世紀科技的預測讓讀者驚嘆不已。

2. With foresight（眞知灼見）

   With foresight, he invested in the emerging market, and it paid off handsomely in the long run. 有著遠見，他在新興市場進行投資，長期來看回報豐厚。

3. Auspicious（好兆頭的）

The rainbow appearing after the storm was seen as an auspicious sign for their journey. 風暴過後出現的彩虹被視為他們旅程中的吉祥兆頭。

4. A prophetic token（好預兆）

Finding an old family heirloom before the big event felt like a prophetic token of good luck. 在重大事件前找到一件古老的家族傳世寶物感覺像是個好運的預兆。

Prescient的同義字詞

1. Foreseeing（預見的／未卜先知的）

Her knack for foreseeing market trends made her a successful investor. 她對市場趨勢的敏感使她成為一位成功的投資者。

2. Prophetic（預言的）

His prophetic dreams often contained clues about future events. 他的預言性夢境常常包含有關未來事件的線索。

3. Predictive（預測的）

The predictive algorithms used in weather forecasting have improved accuracy. 天氣預報中使用的預測算法提高了準確性。

4. Foresighted（有遠見的）

Their foresighted planning allowed them to navigate the challenges effectively. 他們的有遠見的計劃使他們能夠有效應對挑戰。

5. Clairvoyant（通靈的／千里眼的）

Some people claim to have clairvoyant abilities that let them see the future. 一些人聲稱擁有通靈能力，可以看到未來。

Privy | 內情人士透露

Privy是形容詞，知情的、知內情、內幕的，表示某人對某事（內情）有了解或知曉。常用片語為be privy to對某事知（內）情，例如：She was privy to insider information.他了解內幕消息。同義詞片語in the know、in the loop、aware of the situation。

以下來看一些應用的例句

1. I am not privy to their plans, so I can't tell you what they're up to. 我對於他們的計劃並不知情，所以我不能告訴你他們將要做什麼。

2. He is a high-ranking government official and is privy to detailed knowledge of future policy and budget planning direction. 他是黨政高層，對於未來政策及預算規劃的方向知之甚詳。

3. Only a few people are privy to the contents of this classified document. 只有少數人對這個機密文件的內容知情。

RAW-a delightful culinary arts experience
一次RAW令人愉悅的烹飪美食藝術體驗

來認識閱讀美食評論文章前必須知道的單字：

1. Savor（動詞）：品味或享受食物、飲料等的滋味。在這句子中，指的是品味RAW餐廳的美食。

2. Precede（動詞）：在時間、順序或地位上位於前面或在之前發生。這裡指的是RAW餐廳的聲譽在其他事物之前就已經建立起來。

3. Array（名詞）：一系列、一組或一排事物的排列或集合。在這句中，表示夏季菜單包含多道不同的菜餚。

4. Tender（形容詞）：指食物質地柔軟、嫩的，容易咀嚼或切割。

5. Flavorful（形容詞）：意指食物或飲料具有豐富濃郁的風味，美味可口。

6. Showcase（動詞）：展示或展現，特別是指展示某物以供欣賞、觀看或評價。

7. Bounty（名詞）：豐富的供應或收穫，指的是季節的食材充足。

8. Delectable（形容詞）：意指極為美味、可口的，令人愉悅的味道。

9. Medley（名詞）：指多種不同元素或成分的混合物，通常用於描述多樣性的菜餚。

10. Chocolate foie gras sauce（巧克力鵝肝醬）：一種醬汁，由巧克力和鵝肝等成分混合而成，用於搭配肉類或主菜。

11. Delightful（形容詞）：令人愉悅的、令人高興的，表示食物或用餐體驗非常愉快。

12. Culinary（形容詞）：與烹飪或烹飪藝術相關的，指的是食物和烹飪方面的。

13. Zucchini（名詞）：南瓜或夏南瓜，一種蔬菜，通常用於烹飪和料理。

14. Encapsulate（動詞）：簡潔地表達或包含，將某事物或概念縮短並總結。

15. Visual and gustatory delights：Visual視覺上的享受，gustatory味覺上的享受，組指的是將美食的外觀和味道兩方面都納入享受的體驗。

16. Impeccable（形容詞）：完美無瑕的、毫無缺點的，表示服務非常出色且沒有瑕疵。

Today, I had the opportunity to savor RAW, the renowned Michelin-starred restaurant's latest seasonal summer menu. RAW's reputation precedes it, with both the head chef and the restaurant's performance being widely recognized.

中午來嚐嚐米其林餐廳RAW的最新換季夏季菜單，RAW的名氣已經無須多言，主廚和餐廳的表現有目共睹。

The summer set menu, 'The one & only,' featured a delightful array of dishes. The appetizers included tender and flavorful tuna belly with fish skin, and a creamy sea urchin roll wrapped in pork back fat. The 'French-style scrambled egg burrata' made with vegetable oil had a unique airy texture. Various algae offerings provided a taste of the sea, while a medley of summer squash showcased the season's bounty. The combination of semi-raw prawns, sweet shrimp, and lobster, served with Italian rice, offered a juicy and delectable taste that truly captured the essence of summer.

今天夏季套餐The one & only前菜鮪魚中腹和魚皮、豬背脂海膽捲，口感香郁滑嫩；植物油做成的「法式炒蛋布拉塔」像麻糬，吃起來有點空氣感；Algae各式海洋海藻，遍嚐大海的味道；Squash綜合瓜類；還有介於生熟的小蝦、甜蝦及龍蝦，搭配義大利米食，味道鮮美多汁，夏天就是這樣的感覺。

The main course, a steak, was rich in flavor and paired perfectly with grains and a special chocolate foie gras sauce. The artful presentation of the artichoke dish evoked a sense of France, with hints of zucchini and taro, delivering a fresh and delightful culinary experience.

主餐牛排也是味道豐富，搭配穀米、特製巧克力鵝肝醬，層次分明美味，朝鮮薊花料理光看就美不勝收，濃郁的法國風味，吃起來有櫛瓜、芋頭的感覺，很新鮮的體驗和吃法。

In summary, the entire meal beautifully encapsulated the essence of summer through both visual and gustatory delights. The service was warm and impeccable, making it an outstanding dining experience that I highly recommend!

整體而言就是完整演繹夏天的味道，視覺和味覺的饗宴，服務親切、完整，絕佳體驗非常推薦！

Recompense｜補償／報答

Recompense是名詞也可以當動詞，意思是報酬、賠償、報答或補償。一種填補概念，像是Offenders should recompense their victims.犯罪者應賠償受害者。

以下列出例句應用說明

1. The company offered generous recompense to the employees affected by the unexpected layoffs. 公司對突然裁員影響的員工提供了慷慨的賠償。

2. She sought legal recompense for the damage to her property caused by the construction next door. 她尋求法律賠償，因為隔壁的建設損害了她的財產。

3. As a token of appreciation, he sent a small gift to recompense his friend for helping him move. 作為感激之情，他送了一份小禮物以報答朋友幫助他搬家。

4. The company offered recompense to the customers affected by the product recall. 公司向受影響的顧客提供了產品召回的補償。

與報酬或補償有關的單字

1. Remunerate：指的是支付工資、薪水或其他形式的報酬，通常用於工作或勞務。

   The company will remunerate employees for their overtime

FancyEnglish 精湛英文

work. 公司將支付員工的加班工資。

2. Reciprocate：強調互相的回應或回報一個行為或感情。

   When someone is kind to you, it's polite to reciprocate with kindness. 當有人對你好時，以善意回應是有禮貌的。

3. Compensate：泛指補償或賠償，可以包括金錢、物品或服務等，以彌補損失或不便。

   The insurance company will compensate you for the damage to your car. 保險公司將賠償您汽車的損壞。

4. Requite：較少常見，表示報答或回報一種情感、善意或行為。通常帶有一種深情或感激的意味。

   His loyalty and friendship were requited with unwavering support. 他的忠誠和友情得到了堅定的支持以作回報。

5. Reward：指的是對於某種行為、努力或成就所給予的獎勵或報酬。通常用於正面的情境。

   She received a cash reward for winning the competition. 她因贏得比賽而獲得現金獎勵。

以上這些詞彙都涉及報酬或補償，但它們在特定情境中有不同的用法和強調。

Savant｜行家

Savant是名詞，指一位在某一領域或學科方面具有卓越知識或技能的人。來看看以下例句：She is a savant when it comes to playing the violin. 她在拉小提琴方面是一位行家。

來看一下Privy在有關「天然鑽石跌價」的文章中如何運用：Based on individuals privy to the matter, the current price of natural diamonds is plummeting akin to a free fall. Over the past year, De Beers, the world's largest diamond merchant, has significantly reduced prices for some diamonds by over 40%. 來自瞭解內情的人士透露，目前天然鑽石的價格正在急遽下降，猶如自由落體一般。根據報導，過去一年中，全球最大的鑽石商戴比爾斯已將某些鑽石的價格下調超過40%。

相似的字詞和造句：

1. Prodigy（神童）

   The young pianist was a prodigy, playing complex compositions flawlessly. 這位年輕的鋼琴家是一位神童，能夠完美演奏複雜的樂曲。

2. Genius（天才）

   Albert Einstein was a genius in the field of theoretical physics. 阿爾伯特·愛因斯坦在理論物理領域是一位天才。

FancyEnglish 精湛英文

3. Maestro（大師）

The maestro conducted the orchestra with great skill and passion. 這位大師以極高的技巧和熱情指揮著樂團。

4. Virtuoso（大師）

She was a virtuoso on the violin, captivating audiences with her performances. 她是一位小提琴大師，運用她的表演瘋迷聆聽的觀眾。

Scaremonger | 販賣恐懼

Scaremonger可以是名詞或動詞，危言聳聽者、散布令人恐懼的言論者，指那些散播不實訊息或誇大恐懼的人。

閱讀以下報導，學習Scaremonger的在短文之中的應用：
Some critics argue that certain media outlets are scaremongering by sensationalizing the kindergarten medication incident. Concerning inaccurate data and dissemination, this has led to parental panic, prompting lawmakers to urge law enforcement agencies to investigate the matter promptly.
一些批評者認為，某些媒體以危言聳聽的方式渲染幼兒園的餵藥事件，成為恐懼煽動者。關於不正確的資訊和傳播，這導致家長感到恐慌，促使立法者敦促執法機構迅速調查此事。

可以實際應用的例子

The politician was accused of being a scaremonger when he spread false rumors about the economy collapsing. 這位政治家因散布關於經濟崩潰的虛假謠言而被指責為危言聳聽者。

Scaremonger的同義字

Alarmist危言聳聽者，形容那些容易誇大或過度警告某種情況或問題，使人感到不必要的擔憂或恐慌的人。

1. The alarmist headlines in the news were causing unnecessary panic among the public. 新聞中的危言聳聽的標題在公眾中引起了不必要的恐慌。

2. This public figure is often a habitual alarmist; every time the weather gets a little colder, he warns everyone that the Earth is on the verge of an ice age. 這位名嘴常是位習慣性危言聳聽者的人，每次天氣稍微變冷，他就會警告大家，地球即將陷入一場冰河期。

3. In this example, alarmist refers to someone who is overly sensitive to changes in the weather and frequently issues unnecessary warnings. 在這個例子中，alarmist指的是那些對天氣變化過於敏感並且經常發出不必要警告的人。

Serendipity │偶然

Serendipity名詞，指意外發現或偶然發生的幸運事件或情況。通常用來描述一些令人愉快的意外或不可預測的機會。

來看看下面這段短文：

In response to inquiries, officials have expressed the belief that events like the sergeant swimming to China are not coincidental or serendipitous but may be part of a planned conspiracy.

詢問回應時，官方表達了這樣的信念，即像士官游到中國這樣的事件不是巧合或偶然的，而可能是一個有計劃的陰謀的一部分。

應用Serendipity的例句

1. I had a serendipity when I found my childhood toy while cleaning the attic. 當我清理閣樓時，我偶然發現了我的童年玩具，真是個意外的幸運。

2. Their unexpected encounter on the train platform led to a beautiful serendipity, and now they're happily married. 他們在火車站的意外相遇帶來了美麗的偶然，現在他們幸福地結婚了。

3. Serendipity often plays a significant role in scientific discoveries. 偶然通常在科學發現中扮演重要的角色。

Serendipity的同義詞及例句

1. Coincidence（巧合）

   Meeting my old friend at the Eiffel Tower was just a coincidence. 在艾菲爾鐵塔遇見我的老朋友只是一個巧合。

2. Happenstance（偶然）

   Our encounter in that small cafe was pure happenstance. 我們在那家小咖啡館的相遇純粹是偶然。

3. Fortuity（偶然事件）

   Winning the lottery was a fortuity that changed my life. 中獎彩票是改變我生活的偶然事件。

4. Stroke of luck（幸運事件）

   Finding a parking spot right in front of the restaurant was a real stroke of luck. 在餐廳前面找到停車位真是一次真正的幸運事件。

5. Fluke（僥倖）

   His victory in the game was considered a fluke, as he had never won before. 他在遊戲中的勝利被認為是僥倖，因為他以前從未贏過。

6. Providence（天意）

   Some believe that everything happens for a reason and is guided by providence. 有些人相信一切皆有原因，並受到天意的指導。

Effeminate、Sissy | 娘娘腔

「娘娘腔」的英文可以是effeminate或sissy，這兩個詞彙有些微差異，且有時具有貶低含義，具體使用取決於情境。以下是它們的使用情境以及翻譯：

Sissy

有時用來形容一個男性表現出女性特質或行為，通常帶有貶低或輕視的含義。它可能用於嘲笑或侮辱的語境。

1. He was called a sissy because he didn't want to play rough sports with the other boys. 他被叫做娘娘腔，因為他不想和其他男孩一起玩粗野的運動。

2. Don't use sissy as an insult; it's important to be respectful of everyone's personality and expression. 不要把sissy當成一種侮辱；尊重每個人的性格和表達方式很重要。

Effeminate

形容男性展現出女性特質，但沒有像sissy那麼強烈的貶低感。它可以被用來描述某人的外貌、行為方式或風格。

1. His effeminate mannerisms and refined taste in fashion made him stand out in the crowd. 他女性化的舉止和對時尚的精緻品味讓他在人群中顯得與眾不同。

2. He's often teased by his friends for being effeminate. 他經常因為表現娘娘腔而被朋友戲弄。

也就是說Sissy常常帶有貶低或嘲笑的色彩，而Effeminate則較中性，更常用來描述外貌或行為方式，並不一定帶有輕視的含義。但無論使用哪個詞彙，都應謹慎，以避免冒犯他人。

Snap｜折斷／發火／閃快門

來學一個常常搞不清楚的單字Snap，常常在報章雜誌上會閱讀到，但是因為應用的方式多所以，今天拿出來分析一下。

Snap有多種意思，根據上下文不同可以表示不同的詞性和情境。以下一些常見的意思：

1. 名詞：指的是突然的斷裂聲音或拍照聲音。

   I heard a loud snap when the tree branch broke. 樹枝斷裂時我聽到一聲巨響。

2. 動詞：表示突然用力折斷或快速合上。

   She snapped the pencil in half out of frustration. 她因為沮喪將鉛筆折斷。

3. 動詞：表示突然發火、生氣、或反應強烈。

   He snapped at me when I asked him a simple question. 當我問了他一個簡單的問題時，他對我發火了。

4. 名詞：指的是瞬間的快照或簡短的時間段。

   I took a quick snap of the beautiful sunset. 我迅速拍下了美麗的日落快照。

最近一則新聞中，這裡的Snap指的是什麼呢？

A 67-year-old male motorcyclist surnamed Lin was riding through the first section of Zhongshan North Road in Taipei this morning when a sidewalk tree suddenly snapped and collapsed, striking the rider directly on the head. Emergency services arrived at the scene and transported the injured individual to the hospital. Prior to being taken to the hospital, Mr. Lin had no pulse or respiration. The cause of the incident is yet to be determined. Authorities have reported that in the early afternoon, around 1 o'clock, due to the severity of his injuries, Mr. Lin was pronounced dead.

67歲林姓男機車騎士今天近上午行經台北市中山北路一段時，人行道路樹忽然斷掉倒塌，直接砸中騎士頭部。警消到場將傷者送醫，林男送醫前無呼吸心跳，事發原因待釐清。警消指出，騎士下午1時多因傷勢過重宣告不治。

Snap（拍照），同義字Take a photo、Capture an image

1. Take a snap：She decided to take a snap of the beautiful landscape. 她決定拍攝這美麗的風景。
2. Take a photo：I'm going to take a photo of the beautiful sunset. 我要拍下美麗的日落照片。
3. Capture an image：Let's capture an image of this historic landmark. 我們來捕捉這個歷史地標的影像。

Snap（斷裂），同義字Crack、Break apart

1. The branch made a loud snap as it broke apart.樹枝在斷裂時發出巨響的聲音。
2. Crack：She heard a loud crack as the tree branch broke in the storm. 在風暴中，她聽到樹枝斷裂的巨響。

3. Brake apart：He used a hammer to break apart the large rock into smaller pieces. 他用錘子將大石頭打碎成小塊。

Snap（生氣），同義字Lose one's temper、Get angry

1. He snapped when his plans were suddenly changed. 當他的計劃突然改變時，他發火了。

2. Lose one's temper：When she discovered that her little brother had broken her favorite toy, she lost her temper and started shouting. 當她發現她的小弟弟把她最喜歡的玩具弄壞了，她發脾氣並開始大喊大叫。

3. Get angry：He got angry when his colleague repeatedly interrupted him during the important meeting. 在重要會議期間，他的同事反覆打斷他時，他生氣了。

Snap（快速抓住）

1. Capture：He was able to capture the perfect moment with his camera. 他能夠用相機捕捉到完美的時刻。

2. Seize：She seized the opportunity to take a stunning photo. 她抓住了機會拍了一張令人驚嘆的照片。

3. Snatch：He snatched a quick photo of the celebrity as they walked by. 他趁著名人走過時搶拍了一張照片。

4. Grasp：The photographer grasped the chance to get a shot of the rare bird. 攝影師把握住機會拍攝到這隻稀有的鳥。

5. Nab：She nabbed a shot of the beautiful sunset before it disappeared. 她在太陽落山前抓拍到了美麗的日落。

6. Secure：He secured a photograph of the historical monument during his visit.元他在參觀時獲得了一張歷史紀念物的照片。

7. Snap up：Tourists quickly snapped up all the postcards at the souvenir shop. 遊客迅速搶購了紀念品店的所有明信片。

8. Grab：I managed to grab a shot of the fast-moving race car. 我成功地拍下了快速移動的賽車。

希望以上解析和例子更有助於您更深入理解「Snap」的不同表達方式！

Snark｜尖酸刻薄

Snark名詞，指一種帶有諷刺的風格或語調。用來形容言語或行為中的尖刻和嘲笑。

來閱讀一篇Snarky Demands for MRT Priority Seats的短文：
In the world of public transportation, MRT priority seats often face snarky demands. Commuters, eager to secure these coveted spots, sometimes resort to wit over courtesy. These seats, designated for those in need, become battlegrounds for passive-aggressive exchanges. Snarky comments and sarcastic remarks create discomfort. Please remember, let's foster empathy, not snark.

在大眾運輸中，捷運優先座位經常遭到尖酸刻薄的要求。乘客爭搶這些座位，有時用機智勝過禮貌。這些座位為有需要者而設，成為被動攻擊的場所。尖酸刻薄的評論令人不適。請記得，讓我們培養同情心，而不是尖酸刻薄。

請參閱以下應用的例句

1. Her snarky comments about his fashion choices annoyed him. 她對他的時尚選擇發表了尖酸刻薄的評論，讓他感到惱怒。

2. The article was full of snark, making fun of celebrities and their antics. 這篇文章充滿了諷刺，嘲笑名人和他們的滑稽

行爲。

3. Instead of offering constructive feedback, he responded with snark and sarcasm. 他沒有提供建設性的反饋，而是用尖刻和諷刺來回應。

Snark通常用來描述一種帶有挖苦或諷刺意味的言語或態度，通常在批評、幽默或評論中使用。

Snark的同義詞以及應用

1. Sarcasm使用諷刺的語調來嘲笑或嘲弄。

His sarcasm was evident when he saidOh, great job!with a smirk. 當他帶著冷笑說「哦，做得好！」時，他的諷刺顯而易見。

2. Mockery以嘲笑或嘲弄的言語或行爲來嘲笑或挪揄。

Her mockery of his accent was unkind and hurtful. 她對他口音的嘲諷，是不友善和令人受傷的。

3. Irony使用言語或語調，通常是反話，以嘲笑或達諷刺效果。

The irony of the situation was that the fire station burned down. 此情況的諷刺之處在於消防局被燒毀了。

4. Derision通常是對某人或某事的輕視或嘲笑。

He couldn't bear the derision from his classmates any longer. 他再也無法忍受同學們的嘲笑。

Stalemate | 僵持不下

「僵持不下」可以用deadlock或stalemate表達。表示雙方或多方在某個問題上無法達成共識，導致局面陷入僵持，難以有所進展或決策。

來看兩岸僵局造成旅遊提出抗議，及總統選舉在野大聯盟團結造成僵局引發擔憂的短文：

After the COVID-19 pandemic in China, the reopening of outbound tourism excludes Taiwan from the list. Travel operators argue that the political stalemate between the two sides has led to a deadlock, sacrificing and penalizing the industry. They are now contemplating staging a protest to urge the central government for an opening.

在中國經歷了COVID-19大流行後，重新開放的出境旅遊業務未包含台灣在名單內。旅遊業者認為，兩岸政治立場僵持不下，犧牲和懲罰了該行業。他們現在正在考慮舉行抗議，敦促中央政府開放。

This year's presidential election has seen a 'United Opposition Alliance' struggling to take shape, creating a political stalemate within the opposition camp. Supporters have expressed growing concerns about the lack of unity, which is impacting the electoral prospects.

今年總統大選「在野大聯盟」遲遲無法成形，在野陣營團結造成僵局，讓支持者紛紛表示擔憂，影響選情。

再來看看Stalemate的應用

1. The negotiations between the labor union and management have reached a stalemate, and it's affecting productivity. 工會和管理層的談判陷入了僵局，這對生產力產生了影響。

2. The political stalemate between the two major parties has led to a government shutdown. 兩大政黨之間的政治僵局導致政府關閉。

3. The chess match ended in a stalemate when neither player could make a move without putting their king in danger. 這場象棋比賽以僵局告終，因為兩位玩家都無法移動而不使他們的國王陷入危險。

Stalemate的同義字以及例句應用

1. Deadlock：指在爭論或衝突中雙方都無法達成共識或採取行動的情況。
   The negotiations have reached a deadlock, with neither side willing to compromise. 談判已經陷入僵局，雙方都不願意妥協。

2. Impasse：表示一種無法前進或解決的情況，通常因為難以克服的障礙或分歧。
   The contract negotiations have come to an impasse due to disagreements over terms. 由於對條款存在分歧，合約談判已經陷入僵局。

3. Standoff：對立兩方或多方處於對峙狀態，無法向前或後退。

The standoff between the police and the protesters continued for hours. 警察和抗議者之間的對峙持續了幾個小時。

4. Gridlock：表示交通堵塞或停滯不前。在政治或其他領域中也可表示僵局。

During rush hour, the city often experiences gridlock, making it difficult to get anywhere quickly. 在高峰時段，城市經常發生交通堵塞，使快速抵達任何地方變得困難。

這些詞語都描述了一種僵持不下情況，不同方面或各方之間的衝突或阻礙，難以解決，僵持不下。

A prominent figure in showbiz subpoenaed for her incarceration.

演藝圈大姊大法院傳喚發監執行

一些關於法律上的專用英文

1. 教唆偽造本票Instigate forgery of a promissory note
2. 有價證券Valuable securities
3. 自首The act of turning oneself in or surrendering voluntarily
4. 沒收未償還的犯罪所得Confiscation of unrecovered criminal proceeds
5. 傳喚發監subpoena for the incarceration of her sentence.
6. 定讞判決The judgment finality

來閱讀一下以下的短文：

Ms. Chen, a prominent figure in showbiz, was recently declared guilty of instigating the forgery of a promissory note and possessing valuable securities. She received a three-year prison sentence, while her sister, who voluntarily surrendered, received a suspended sentence.

The highest court issued a final judgment, confirming the guilt and the confiscation of 430,000 yuan in unrecovered criminal proceeds. This judgment finality was upheld by the Supreme Court, and Ms. Chen has been subpoenaed to appear in court for the incarceration of her sentence.

陳女士，一位演藝圈知名人物，最近被宣判有罪，罪名包括教唆偽造本票及有價證券。她被判處三年監禁，而她的姊姊主動自首，獲得緩刑。最高法院最終判確定，沒收43萬元的未追回的犯罪所得。最終判決最高法院確認，陳女士傳喚發監執行。

Temerity │ 魯莽／冒失

Temerity魯莽、冒失，描述某人做出冒險或不顧後果的行為時使用。

以下是句子的應用

1. She had the temerity to challenge the boss's decision in front of the entire team. 她竟然在整個團隊面前挑戰老闆的決定，實在太魯莽了。

2. It takes a lot of temerity to skydive for the first time without any training. 第一次嘗試跳傘且沒有接受過任何培訓，需要相當的冒失。

3. His temerity in asking his crush out on a date, even though they had just met, was surprising. 他竟然在剛認識不久的情況下，向心儀的人約會，這種行為令人驚訝。

Temerity的一些同義詞

1. Audacity（大膽）
   She had the audacity to ask for a raise after only a month on the job. 她竟然在工作不到一個月時大膽地要求加薪。

2. Rashness（輕率）
   His rashness in making decisions without considering the consequences often led to problems. 他在不考慮後果的情況下做決定的輕率態度常常引發問題。

3. Impetuosity（衝動、魯莽）

His impetuosity got the better of him, and he quit his job without a backup plan. 他的衝動使他失去理智，毫無後備計劃地辭去了工作。

4. Recklessness（魯莽行爲）

His recklessness while driving resulted in a serious accident. 他駕車的魯莽行爲導致了一起嚴重的事故。

5. Boldness（大膽）

Her boldness in presenting new ideas impressed her colleagues. 她大膽提出新想法，給同事留下了深刻印象。

以上是一些與Temerity相同意思的同義詞，它們都指的是在行動或言談中表現出的魯莽、冒失、大膽或不考慮後果的特質。

Tenuous | 脆弱

Tenuous形容詞，纖弱的、脆弱的、稀薄的或不堅固的。用來描述某物的物理或抽象特性，指其稀薄、脆弱或不牢固的程度。

應用例句

1. The tenuous thread holding the fragile vase snapped, and it shattered on the floor. 支撐易碎花瓶的纖弱線斷了，它摔碎在地板上。

2. Her tenuous connection with her distant relatives meant that she didn't know them well. 她與遠親之間的淡薄聯繫意味著她不太了解他們。

3. The company's tenuous financial situation forced it to cut costs and lay off employees. 公司脆弱的財務狀況迫使它削減成本並裁減員工。

Tenuous的同義詞

1. 薄弱的（Fragile）：容易破碎或崩潰的。
   The fragile bridge couldn't support heavy traffic. 這座脆弱的橋無法支撐重車流量。

2. 虛弱的（Weak）：缺乏力量或穩定性的。
   His weak argument couldn't convince anyone. 他虛弱的論點無法說服任何人。

3. 不牢固的（Unstable）：缺乏穩定性或堅固性的。

The chair felt unstable, and she almost fell. 這把椅子感覺不穩，她差點摔倒。

4. 纖細的（Delicate）：非常細小或需要輕柔處理的。

The delicate porcelain vase should be handled with care. 這個纖細的瓷花瓶應該小心處理。

5. 貧弱的（Feeble）：缺乏必要的資源、支持或力量的。

His feeble attempts at fixing the car only made it worse. 他軟弱的嘗試修車只讓情況變得更糟。

The scam is rampant.
| 詐騙猖獗

Scam名詞，詐騙行爲，指欺騙人們錢財或財物的不誠實行爲。Rampant是形容詞，表示某事物情況非常普遍、嚴重、橫行無阻。以下是分別針對Scam和Rampant舉的例子：

Scam

1. They got involved in an online scam and lost all of their savings. 他們參與了一椿線上詐騙，失去了所有的儲蓄。
2. The email claimed you won a prize, but it was actually a scam. 該電子郵件聲稱您中了一個獎品，但實際上只是一椿詐騙。
3. The police are investigating this investment scam scheme that has affected hundreds of people. 警方正在調查這個投資詐騙計劃，數百人受害。

Rampant

1. Crime has become rampant in this city, and citizens are concerned for their safety. 犯罪在這個城市變得猖獗，市民擔心自己的安全。
2. Spam emails and online scams are rampant on the internet and difficult to control. 垃圾郵件和網絡詐騙在網絡上猖獗，難以控制。

3. Unregulated logging has led to rampant destruction of the forests. 無篩選的伐木導致了森林猖獗的破壞。

Scam和Rampant的同義詞

1. Fraud（詐騙）

There has been a surge in online fraud cases. 網上詐騙案件大幅增加。

2. Deception（欺騙／詐欺）

The company was involved in a massive deception of its customers. 該公司涉及大規模欺詐其顧客。

3. Swindle（欺騙）

He swindled innocent people out of their savings. 他欺騙了無辜的人們的儲蓄。

Rampant的同義詞

1. Widespread（普遍的）

Corruption is widespread in that region. 該地區腐敗問題普遍存在。

2. Pervasive（普及的）

The smell of pollution is pervasive in the city. 城市中充斥著污染的氣味。

3. Ubiquitous（無處不在的）

Smartphones have become ubiquitous in modern society. 智慧手機在現代社會無處不在。

Travesty │ 鬧劇一場

Travesty名詞，嘲諷、歪曲。常用來針對某個事物或主題與事實乖離表示「歪曲或嘲諷」某種荒謬或草率的行為或表現；或是形容一種「滑稽、模仿劇、鬧劇」。

In the eyes of some, judicial reform is nothing more than a travesty.在某些人的眼中司法改革只不過是一場鬧劇。

一些相關同義詞

「嘲諷」satire、derision、mockery、ridicule、farcicality、jocularity；「歪曲」distortion、warp；
「滑稽喜劇／鬧劇」farce、burlesque、parody、lampoon、caricature

Travesty的英文例句應用範例

1. The movie's portrayal of historical events was a complete travesty, as it distorted the facts and turned them into a farcical comedy. 這部電影對歷史事件的描繪完全是一種歪曲，因為它扭曲了事實並將它們變成了一齣滑稽喜劇。

2. The unfair trial and wrongful conviction of an innocent man was a clear travesty of justice. 對一名無辜男子的不公平審判和誤判是明顯對司法的嘲諷。

3. The political debate turned into a travesty due to all the name-calling and interruptions. 政治辯論因為所有的互相指責和打斷而變成了一場滑稽模仿。

Troll、Internet Brigade
｜酸民／網軍／側翼

網路上的使用者有很多種型態，我們來介紹一下「酸民、網軍及側翼」各種網路使用者英文的說法：

1. Troll（酸民或網絡騷擾者）

   He is a troll who frequently engages in malicious attacks on others on social media.

2. Internet Brigade（網軍）

   The government was accused of using an Internet brigade to manipulate online discussions. 政府被指控使用網軍來操縱線上討論。

   The Internet brigade flooded social media with propaganda during the election. 選舉期間，網軍在社交媒體上洪水般地散播宣傳。

3. Online army（網軍）

   The online army of trolls was responsible for spreading misinformation during the election. 選舉期間，網軍的惡意評論者負責散布虛假訊息。

   Governments in some countries have been known to deploy an online army to manipulate public opinion. 一些國家的政府已知使用網軍來操控公眾意見。

側翼、政黨側翼或網軍的英文術語

1. Flanker側翼：Flank通常表示在戰術上包圍或進行側翼攻擊的行為。「網路上側翼」則為Flanker、Flanking cyber army、Online flanker或Internet Flanker。

2. Faction Party派系：Faction party可能是指政治上的派系，用於描述內部政黨中的不同派系。

3. Wing Party派系：Wing party通常我們使用wing來描述政黨的不同派系，例如left-wing party表示左派政黨，right-wing party 表示右派政黨。

來看一下短文中的應用：

The leader of a certain political party claims that the presidential candidate from the ruling party has never faced journalists; instead, spokespersons, online armies, Internet flankers, and pundits are the ones engaged in political discourse.

某政黨領袖宣稱執政黨總統參選人從來都不面對記者，都是發言人、網軍、側翼、名嘴出面來進行打政治攻防。

其他網路使用者介紹

1. Netizen（網友）

This website attracts thousands of netizens who share their views and opinions. 這個網站吸引了成千上萬的網友分享他們的觀點和意見。

2. Cybercitizen（網絡公民）

As a cybercitizen, we have a responsibility to follow the rules and ethical guidelines on the internet. 作為一位網絡公民，

我們有責任遵守網路上的規則和道德準則。

3. Online user（在線用戶）

The number of online users reached its peak in the evening.
晚上在線用戶數量達到了巔峰。

4. Provocateurs（煽動者）

Some internet provocateurs try to sow division and discord.
一些網絡煽動者試圖製造分裂和不和。

5. Flambait（挑釁）

He enjoys flambaiting others and provoking arguments online.
他喜歡挑釁別人，引起爭論。

6. Internet troublemaker（網絡麻煩製造者）

There's an internet troublemaker on this forum who often
causes chaos. 這個論壇上有個網絡麻煩製造者，經常引起
混亂。

7. Gossip（八卦）

She loves spreading gossip online and always knows other
people's secrets. 她喜歡在網路上散播八卦而且總是知道別
人的祕密。

8. Nitpicker（吹毛求疵者）

He's a nitpicker, always finding minor flaws in everything
posted online.他真是個吹毛求疵的人，總是能找到網路上
所有發布的事情中的小毛病。

9. Stirrer（煽風點火者）

He's a stirrer who likes to create trouble within an on group.
他是個煽風點火的人，喜歡在群體內製造麻煩。

Truculent | 好鬥兇猛

Truculent形容詞，形容人或動物表現出好戰、攻擊性強烈、咄咄逼人的特質。

來看看以下Truculent的例句

1. The truculent dog barked fiercely at anyone who approached its territory. 那隻兇猛的狗對任何接近它領地的人都兇狠地吠叫。
2. During the argument, his truculent attitude made it difficult to find a peaceful resolution. 在爭論中，他好鬥的態度使得難以找到和平解決的方法。
3. The boxer's truculent demeanor in the ring intimidated his opponents. 拳擊手在拳擊場上兇猛的風格嚇到了對手。

Truculent的同義詞，以及相應的英文例句和翻譯

1. Aggressive（好鬥的）
   The aggressive driver cut off other cars on the highway. 那位好鬥的司機在高速公路上擅自變換車道。
2. Belligerent（好戰的）
   The belligerent nations were engaged in a long-standing conflict. 那些好戰的國家捲入了長期的衝突。
3. Hostile（敵對的）
   Her hostile attitude towards her colleagues created tension in

the workplace. 她對同事敵對的態度在工作場所造成了緊張。

4. Mlitant（好戰的）

The militant protesters demanded immediate political change. 激進的抗議者要求立即政治改變。

5. Pugnacious（愛爭吵的）

His pugnacious nature often led to heated arguments with his friends. 他愛爭吵的性格常常與朋友引發激烈爭論。

都表示強烈的、好戰的單字

1. Truculent（好鬥的）

The truculent bull charged at the matador with fury in its eyes. 那頭好鬥的公牛帶著狂怒的眼神向鬥牛士衝去。

2. Intrepid（無畏的）

The intrepid explorer ventured deep into the uncharted jungle, fearless of the dangers that lay ahead. 那位無畏的探險家深入未經探索的叢林，對前方的危險毫不畏懼。

3. Ferocious（兇猛的）

The ferocious storm unleashed its full fury, causing widespread destruction. 兇猛風暴釋放了它全部的狂怒，造成廣泛的破壞。

4. Bellicose（好戰的）

The bellicose nation threatened its neighbors with military action. 那個好戰的國家威脅要對其鄰國進行軍事行動。

FancyEnglish 精湛英文

Intrepid、ferocious、bellicose及undaunted用法和語氣上略與Truculent不同，Truculent更強調攻擊性和好戰，intrepid強調無畏和勇敢，ferocious強調兇猛和狂怒，而bellicose更偏向描述國家或集體的好戰特質。

Truculent和Undaunted的語氣和用法略有不同

Truculent：強調好戰、攻擊性或咄咄逼人的態度，帶有更多的負面意義，暗示對抗或衝突。

Undaunted：強調對困難、危險或挑戰的無畏，形容人在面對逆境或困難時保持勇敢、堅定和不屈不撓的態度。

US demands halt to unscrupulous China cyber-spying. 美國要求停止「不擇手段」的中國網絡間諜活動。

Unscrupulous
| 不檢點的／不道德的

Scrupulous謹慎的、細心的，形容人或行為的謹慎，有良好的道德標準。反義詞Unscrupulous（不檢點的、不道德的）指為達目的不擇手段、不顧及道德倫理。

運用在綠能話題：

The chairman of the green energy industry resigned from his position, accusing his opponents of using unscrupulous means to efface his political credentials as a tool in their political struggle, which is undesirable for the long-term development trends of the green energy sector.

綠能產業的董事長辭去職務，指控他的對手不擇手段，以抹滅他的政治資歷作為他們政治鬥爭的工具，這對綠能產業長期發展趨勢是不可取的。（註：Efface抹去、擦掉、消除。）

Unscrupulous的同義字

包括Dishonest、Deceitful、Unethical、Unprincipled、Amoral、Immoral等。

我們來看一下例句

1. The unscrupulous businessman exploited legal loopholes to

avoid paying taxes. 那位不道德的商人利用法律漏洞避免支付稅款。

2. She encountered unscrupulous individuals who tried to scam her out of her savings. 她遇到了不檢點的人，試圖騙她的儲蓄。

3. The politician was accused of engaging in unscrupulous behavior during the election campaign. 這位政治家被指控在選舉活動期間參與不檢點的行為。

4. The whistleblower revealed a series of unscrupulous activities within the organization. 這名告密者揭示了該組織內部的一系列不道德活動。

Under the weather
身體不適

Under the weather描述身體不舒服、健康狀況不佳時。

Under the weather英文句子及應用

1. I can't come to work today; I'm feeling a bit under the weather. 我今天無法上班；我感覺有點不適。
2. She's been under the weather for the past few days, so she's staying home to rest. 她過去幾天一直身體不適，所以她待在家休息。
3. Don't expect him to be very productive today; he's sick and definitely under the weather. 別指望他今天會很有產出；他生病了，肯定不適。

Under the weather的同義詞和片語

1. Feeling unwell（感覺不適）：形容身體狀況不好，通常與輕微的生病或不適有關。

   Feeling unwell: She called in sick to work because she was feeling unwell. 她因感到不舒服而請病假不去工作。
2. Sick（生病）：身體出現疾病症狀，需要休息或醫療照顧。

   I can't go to the party tonight; I am feeling sick with a fever. 我今晚不能參加派對；我發燒感到生病。

3. Out of sorts（情緒不佳）：情緒上感到不舒服或心情糟糕。

After a sleepless night, he was feeling out of sorts and irritable.
一夜未眠，他感到情緒不佳且易怒。

Unkempt | 蓬頭垢面

Unkempt形容詞，不整潔的、凌亂的。形容外表或狀態很混亂、不整齊或不潔淨，蓬頭垢面。

英文例句

1. The abandoned house had an unkempt garden with overgrown weeds and wild bushes. 這個廢棄的房子前庭有座長滿野草和野叢的不整潔花園。

2. She woke up with her hair all tangled and unkempt after a restless night. 她一夜難眠，早上醒來頭髮亂糟糟的，一點也不整潔。

3. His unkempt appearance at the job interview left a bad impression on the interviewer. 他面試時不整潔的外表給面試官留下了不好的印象。

Unkempt的同義字

1. Disheveled（凌亂的）衣冠不整，毛髮凌亂。

   Her hair was so disheveled that it looked like she had just woken up. 她的頭髮凌亂不堪，看起來像是剛剛醒來一樣。

2. Untidy（不整潔的）缺乏整潔，雜亂無章。

   The living room was untidy with toys and books scattered everywhere. 客廳一片雜亂，到處都是散落的玩具和書本。

 FancyEnglish 精湛英文

3. Rumpled（皺巴巴的）像被壓皺的一樣。

He emerged from bed with rumpled clothes and messy hair. 他從床上起來，衣服皺巴巴，頭髮亂糟糟的。

4. Shabby（破舊的）衣衫襤褸，外表破舊不整潔。

The old man lived in a shabby house that needed extensive repairs. 這位老人住在一間破舊的房子裡，需要大修。

5. Messy（混亂的）指事物或狀態的混亂和不整潔。

The children left a messy trail of crumbs after eating cookies in the kitchen. 孩子們在廚房吃完餅乾後，留下了一條麵包屑的混亂軌跡。

6. Slovenly（邋遢的）形容人的外表或穿著不整潔，缺乏整齊。

She was often criticized for her slovenly appearance at work, as she rarely bothered to dress neatly. 她經常因工作時邋遢的外表而受到批評，因為她很少注意整齊穿著。

7. Cluttered（雜亂的）強調有大量零散物品或物件散布在一個地方，使其看起來混亂。

His desk was cluttered with papers, making it difficult to find anything. 他的書桌上堆滿了文件，讓尋找東西變得困難。

Usurp｜奪權

Usurp動詞，Usurpation名詞，指篡奪的行爲，指非法或越權地奪取權力、地位或地位。指某人或某個團體未經合法程序，試圖取代或篡奪現有的權威。通常有貶義，因爲它暗示了非法或不正當的行爲。

我們來看一下將Usurp套用在有關阿富汗塔利班奪權報導：

On the 2nd anniversary of the Taliban's usurpation, the plight of women's rights in Afghanistan remains unresolved, with local women facing restrictions usurped upon them in public spaces, employment, and education.

塔利班奪權2週年，阿富汗女權慘況未解，當地婦女在公共場所、工作及教育方面受到限制。（註：restrictions usurped upon them in public spaces表示這些限制是以「不合法或強制」的方式加在婦女身上，而不是基於公正或合法的權力。在這種情況下，婦女的權利受到了強制性的侵害。）

Usurp的用法示例

1. The military general attempted to usurp the president's authority by staging a coup. 軍事將軍試圖發動政變，篡奪總統的權威。

2. She managed to usurp the leadership position within the company by manipulating the board of directors. 她成功地透

過操縱董事會，篡取了公司的領導職位。

3. The ambitious nobleman plotted to usurp the throne and become the new king. 這位野心勃勃的貴族策劃著篡奪王位，成為新國王。

Usurp的同義字及例句

1. Seize（奪取）強行或突然地取得權力、地位或控制權。
   He tried to seize control of the company by buying up all the shares. 他試圖通過購買所有的股份來奪取公司的控制權。

2. Appropriate（占用，據為己有）非法或不當取得某物或某權。
   The dictator appropriated the country's resources for his personal gain. 獨裁者為了個人利益占用了該國的資源。

3. Overthrow（推翻）推翻現有的政權或領導地位。
   The rebels sought to overthrow the oppressive regime. 反叛分子試圖推翻壓迫性的政權。

4. Supplant（取而代之）強調取代某人或某事。
   The new technology could supplant the old method of production. 新技術可能取代舊的生產方法。

5. Sequester（隔離，隱藏）為了取得控制權，將某物或某人隔離或隱藏。
   The detective sequestered the evidence until the investigation was complete.警探將證據隔離，直到調查完

6. Usurpation（篡奪）這是usurp的名詞形式，意思相同，指的是非法篡奪或取得權力。

His usurpation of the throne led to a period of political turmoil. 他對王位的篡奪導致了一段政治動盪時期。

7. Usurpation（篡奪）非法取得權力或地位的行爲，通常指政治或權力方面的行爲。

The usurpation of land by the wealthy elite displaced many poor families. 富有的精英對土地的篡奪使許多貧困家庭流離失所。

Vacuous | 空洞愚蠢

Vacuous意指空洞的、無意義的或愚蠢的。用來形容缺乏內容、智慧或深度的事物。通常在批評性的語境中使用。

英文例句

1. Her vacuous expression during the lecture showed that she wasn't paying any attention. 她在講座期間的空洞表情顯示她完全沒在注意。

2. The movie received harsh reviews for its vacuous plot and one-dimensional characters. 這部電影因其空洞的情節和單一維度的角色而受到嚴厲的評價。

3. His vacuous excuses for being late to work were met with skepticism by his boss. 他對於上班遲到的空泛藉口引起了老闆的懷疑。

Vacuous的同義字

1. Empty（空的）

   The room was empty, devoid of any furniture. 這個房間是空的，沒有任何家具。

2. Hollow（空洞的）

   Her promises felt hollow and insincere. 她的承諾聽起來空洞而不真誠。

3. Blank（空白的）

The paper was blank, waiting for the writer's words. 這張紙是空白的，等待著作者的文字。

4. Inane（空洞／無用）

Their conversation was so inane that I couldn't bear to listen. 他們的對話如此愚蠢，我無法忍受聽下去。（註：Inane 愚蠢、空洞、無聊的，用來形容缺乏智慧、深度或意義的事物或言論。）

5. Vapid（平淡的、乏味的）

Sentence: The movie was so vapid that I fell asleep halfway through. 這部電影如此乏味，我半途睡著了。（註：Vapid 乏味的、平淡的或缺乏興趣。當你形容某事物或言論為 vapid 時，你正在指出它缺乏活力、吸引力或深度，太過平庸或無趣。通常用於文學、音樂、電影或對話等方面。）

6. Insipid（平淡的）

The soup tasted insipid, lacking any flavor. 這湯味道平淡，毫無風味。

這些詞都有描述空洞、缺乏深度或意義的意思，可以根據上下文選擇適當的同義詞。

Vacuous 和 Nugatory 都表達了某事物的無價值或無意義性質，但它們的用法和強調有所不同

Vacuous：描述缺乏思想、智慧或深度的事物，強調空洞和缺乏內容。例如，一個 vacuous 笑話可能是毫無趣味或智慧的笑話。

Nugatory：強調某事物的「無關緊要」、無價值、無意義或微不足道，但它有時也可以指向形式上有價值但實際上不重要的事物。常用於法律或正式文件中，表示法律效力微乎其微。

Venerable | 尊敬景仰

Venerable形容詞，形容值得尊敬和敬仰的事物或人。常用於描述長者、歷史悠久的事物、文化傳統、或擁有高度權威的人。

一起來看例句的應用

1. The venerable professor had been teaching at the university for over five decades. 這位受人尊敬的教授在大學教課已經超過五十年了。
2. The ancient temple, with its ornate architecture and rich history, is considered a venerable landmark in the city. 這座古老的寺廟憑藉其華麗的建築和悠久歷史，被認爲是城市中令人景仰的地標。
3. The venerable tradition of storytelling has been passed down through generations, preserving our cultural heritage. 悠久的說故事傳統代代相傳，保存了我們的文化遺產。

Venerable的同義字

1. Respectable（值得尊敬的）：形容那些因爲長期的表現或品德而受到尊敬的人或事物。
   The elderly gentleman is highly respectable in the community. 這位年邁的紳士在社區中非常值得尊敬。
2. Dignified（有尊嚴的）：強調某人事物的優雅和尊貴。

The ceremony was conducted in a dignified manner. 典禮以有尊嚴的方式進行。

3. Honorable（光榮的）：表示某人或事受到榮譽和尊重。

Winning the Nobel Prize is an honorable achievement. 贏得諾貝爾獎是一項光榮的成就。

4. Revered（受尊敬的）：形容那些深受尊敬和崇拜的人事物。

The ancient temple is revered by the local population. 這座古老的寺廟深受當地人民的崇敬。

5. Esteemed（受尊重的）：表示某人事物因其價值而受到重視。

The professor is highly esteemed in the field of physics. 這位教授在物理領域受到高度尊重。

Vicarious
感同身受！（替代或間接的）

Vicarious形容詞，代理的或替代的（情感或經歷的替代）或是間接的，也類似「感同身受的」！但不是自己的親身體驗，通常用來描述透過觀看或體驗他人的經歷、感受或情感來感受某事物。也就是To act, feel, or experience through another person.

He took vicarious pleasure in his son's success. 父親透過兒子成就感同身受，就是有一種替代或是間接感受到的歡愉喜悅的感情觸發。

這邊要注意！Vicarious和感同身受（empathetic或sympathetic）有一定程度的相似性，Vicarious表示通過觀察或經歷他人的事物而感到類似的情感。強調的是一種「間接」的體驗，而不是自身親身經歷。在He took vicarious pleasure in his son's success.中，vicarious意味他通過兒子的成功感到「間接的」愉悅，而不是他自己親自取得了成功。Empathetic或Sympathetic感同身受，更強調自己與他人的「情感共鳴」，通常指的是對他人的情感體驗有深刻理解和共感。這種情感可能是直接的，因為自己也曾經有類似的經歷，也可能是出於同情或關懷。它更注重情感上的共鳴。所以，雖然這些詞都涉及情感共鳴，重點和用法略有不同。

來看一下Vicarious例句

1. She had a vicarious thrill watching her daughter perform on stage.她透過看女兒在舞台上表演，感到一種感情替代的激動。

2. Reading about the adventures of the characters in the book gave him a vicarious sense of excitement. 閱讀書中角色的冒險經歷讓他產生了一種角色替代的興奮感。

3. He lived vicariously through his friend's travels, enjoying the stories and photos shared from around the world. 他透過朋友的旅行，間接地享受著從世界各地分享的故事和照片。

當Vicarious意指「間接的」，同義詞有

1. Indirect（間接的）

He experienced the thrill of the adventure through indirect means. 他透過間接的方式體驗了冒險的刺激。

2. Mediated（中介的）

Their communication was mediated by a translator. 他們的溝通是透過一位翻譯進行的。

當Vicarious意指「代理的」，同義詞有

1. Proxy（代理人）

She acted as a proxy for her boss in the meeting. 她在會議中代表她的老闆行事。

2. Surrogate（替代）

The surrogate mother carried the child for the couple. 代孕媽

媽爲這對夫妻懷孕。

當Vicarious意指「替代的」，同義詞有

1. Substitutive（替代的）

They used a substitutive ingredient in the recipe. 他們在食譜中使用了替代性的成分。

2. Replacement（代替／更換）

The old car was beyond repair and needed a complete replacement. 舊車無法修復，需要完全更換。

當Vicarious意指「以他人經歷爲樂」，同義詞有

1. Experiential（經歷的）

Some people find experiential learning more engaging than vicarious learning. 有些人覺得體驗學習比以他人經歷爲樂的學習方式更吸引人。

2. Secondhand（二手的）

He gained a secondhand understanding of the event through others' accounts. 他透過別人的描述獲得了對事件的間接理解。

當Vicarious意指「情感上代替他人經歷」，同義詞有

1. Empathetic（同理心的）

Her empathetic response to his pain made him feel understood. 她對他的痛苦的同情回應讓他感到被理解。

2. Compassionate（同情的）

The compassionate support from friends served as a vicarious source of strength. 朋友們的同情支持成爲一種情感上的力量來源。

Volatile | 波動不穩

Volatile形容詞，有變動、波動的，用來描述某物或某人容易變化、不穩定、易爆發或情緒波動劇烈的特性。

通常在以下的情境中使用

1. Financial markets can be highly volatile, with stock prices fluctuating rapidly. 金融市場可能非常不穩定，股價波動迅速。

2. She has a volatile temper; you never know when she'll get angry.她的脾氣很火爆，你永遠不知道她什麼時候會生氣。

3. The chemical reaction became volatile, leading to an unexpected explosion. 這個化學反應變得極度不穩定，導致意外爆炸。

Volatile形容物體、情緒或情況不穩定及波動的性質，因此在使用時需要注意上下文，以確保準確表達所描述的不穩定特性。

Volatile的同義詞，以及使用方式

1. Unstable（不穩定的）：指的是容易改變或崩潰的狀態，可能在任何時候出現變化。

   The political situation in the region is highly unstable. 該地區

的政治局勢非常不穩定。

2. Erratic（不穩定的、反覆無常的）：指的是行為或情況不規則、不一致，很難預測。

His erratic driving made the passengers uneasy. 他不穩定的駕駛讓乘客感到不安。

3. Temperamental（喜怒無常的）：指的是情感或性格容易變化，常伴隨著情緒波動。

The artist was known for being temperamental, sometimes creating masterpieces and other times destroying his work. 這位藝術家以喜怒無常而聞名，有時創作傑作，有時毀掉自己的作品。

4. Capricious（反覆無常的、變化無常的）指的是隨意而變的，通常指人或決策容易改變。

The weather in this region can be quite capricious, so it's best to be prepared for sudden changes. 這個地區的天氣變化無常，最好隨時做好應對突變的準備。

Voters on the fence
│ 猶豫不決的選民

來談談選民結構相關的英文。

Undecided voters指那些尚未決定投票給哪一方的選民，但不一定表示他們持中間立場。

Voters on the fence是指尚未做出最終選擇、還在猶豫不決、尚未決定投票給哪一方的選民，這些選民還會透過辯論及政策討論再做一番決定。

On the fence也可以當是否接受offer時「猶豫不決」使用，像 I'm on the fence about whether to accept the job offer because I'm not sure if it aligns with my long-term career goals.

其他樣態的選民

1. 中間選民：Centrist voters
2. 偏右選民：Right-leaning voters
3. 偏左選民：Left-leaning voters
4. 搖擺投票的選民 ：Swing voters
5. 溫和政治立場的選民：Moderate voters
6. 獨立選民：Independent voters指不附屬於特定政黨的選民

Voters on the fence應用的例子

1. The candidates are working hard to sway voters on the fence with their policy proposals and campaign promises. 候選人們

正努力通過他們的政策提案和競選承諾來影響那些猶豫不決的選民。

2. In this swing state, there is a significant number of voters on the fence, making it a critical battleground in the upcoming election. 在這個搖擺州，有相當多的猶豫不決的選民，使它成為即將舉行的選舉中的關鍵戰場。

3. The undecided voters on the fence have been closely following the candidates' debates and interviews to make an informed choice. 這些猶豫不決的選民一直在密切關注候選人的辯論和訪談，以做出明智的選擇。

Welter | 騷動

Welter可做名詞和動詞，根據上下文的不同，意思有所不同。

Welter作名詞時，是混亂或無序的狀態

1. As the storm raged on, the beach was in a welter of debris and seaweed. 當風暴肆虐時，沙灘上一片混亂，滿是碎屑和海草。
2. The sudden news of the company's bankruptcy threw the employees into a welter of confusion and worry. 公司破產的突然消息使員工陷入混亂和擔憂之中。
3. After the intense workout, he lay on the ground weltering in sweat and exhaustion. 經過激烈的運動後，他躺在地上汗流浹背，筋疲力盡。

Welter作動詞時，是使某事物陷入混亂，或在某事物中打滾或翻滾

1. The sudden influx of orders weltered the production team, causing delays in fulfilling customer requests. 突然湧入的訂單使生產團隊陷入混亂，導致無法及時完成客戶的要求。
2. The controversial decision by the board of directors weltered the company's stock price, leading to a sharp decline. 董事會爭議性的決定使公司股價陷入混亂，導致急劇下跌。

3. The unexpected power outage weltered the conference, leaving attendees in the dark and disrupting the entire event. 突然的停電使會議陷入混亂，讓與會者處於黑暗中，擾亂了整個活動。

Welter的名詞同義詞以及例句

1. Chaos（混亂）

   After the protest, the streets were in chaos, with overturned cars and broken windows. 示威過後，街道一片混亂，汽車翻倒，窗戶破碎。

2. Disarray（混亂）

   The unexpected announcement threw the party into disarray as members scrambled to make decisions. 意外的宣布使得黨內一片混亂，成員紛紛爭相做出決策。

3. Tumult（騷動）

   The tumult in the stadium erupted when the home team scored a last-minute goal. 主場隊最後一刻進球時，體育場內爆發了騷動。

4. Confusion（困惑）

   The sudden change in the schedule caused confusion among the passengers at the airport. 行程表的突然變更使機場的乘客感到困惑。

5. Mayhem（大混亂）

   The rioters created mayhem in the city, setting fires and looting stores. 暴民在城市裡製造了大混亂，縱火並搶劫商店。

這些詞都可以用來描述混亂、無秩序或騷動的狀態，根據上下文的不同選擇適當的詞彙。

Welter的動詞同義詞

包括flummox、baffle、confound、perplex和bewilder，都有相似的含義，表示使某人感到困惑、迷惑或無法理解。但需要注意的是，每個單字可能在一些微妙的方面有不同的語義或用法，但在大多數情況下它們可以互換使用。

Wrangle vs Wangle

Wrangle（動詞）爭論、爭吵、爭辯

通常用於描述人們在討論、爭執或爭論某事時的行為。

1. They always seem to wrangle over trivial matters. 他們似乎總是在瑣碎的事情上爭論不休。

2. The politicians wrangled for hours in the debate. 政治家們在辯論中爭論了幾個小時。

3. It's pointless to wrangle about who's to blame; let's find a solution. 爭論誰該負責是毫無意義的，我們應該找到解決辦法。

Wangle（動詞）詭計地取得、狡猾地獲得

通常用於描述某人巧妙地或狡猾地取得或達成某事，通常是在困難或不正當的情況下。

1. He managed to wangle a free ticket to the concert. 他巧妙地弄到了一張免費的音樂會門票。

2. She wangled her way into the exclusive club without an invitation. 她在沒有邀請的情況下巧妙地進入了尊貴俱樂部。

3. It's amazing how he wangled a promotion so quickly. 他如何如此迅速地巧妙地爭取到了升職真是令人驚訝。

Wrangle的同義詞

1. Quarrel爭吵，爭執

   They always quarrel over money matters. 他們總是在金錢問題上爭吵。

2. Argue爭論，爭辯

   They like to argue about politics. 他們喜歡爭論政治。

Wangle的同義詞

1. Contrive：巧妙地安排，策劃

   He contrived a clever way to solve the problem. 他策劃了一個巧妙的方法來解決問題。

2. Juggle：巧妙地應對，處理多項事務

   She had to juggle her job, family, and personal life. 她不得不巧妙地應對工作、家庭和個人生活。

3. Wangle：巧妙地取得，狡猾地獲得

   He wangled a free ticket to the concert. 他巧妙地弄到了一張免費的音樂會門票。

4. Manipulate：操控，操縱

   He managed to manipulate the situation to his advantage. 他成功地操縱了局勢以取得利益。

5. Secure：取得，獲得

   She secured a scholarship to the prestigious university. 她獲得了進入優秀大學的獎學金。

6. Obtain獲得，取得

   He tried to obtain a loan from the bank. 他試圖從銀行獲得貸款。

Zeal Zealous Zealot
| 狂熱份子

分別來說明一下這三個單字的意思和使用情境：

Zeal 熱情，熱忱，熱衷

是用來描述對某事物或目標的強烈興趣和積極性。

1. Her zeal for music is evident in her daily practice. 她對音樂的熱情在她的日常練習中表現出來。
2. His zeal for social justice led him to volunteer at the local shelter. 他對社會正義的熱忱使他志願在當地的庇護所工作。
3. The team's zeal to win the championship was unmatched.這支球隊贏得冠軍的熱情是無與倫比的。

Zealous 熱情的，熱衷的，熱心的

形容某人對某事物或目標表現出強烈的熱情和積極性。

1. She is a zealous advocate for animal rights. 她是一位熱心的動物權益倡導者。
2. The zealous student always volunteered to help with class projects. 這位熱衷的學生總是志願協助課堂項目。
3. His zealous dedication to his work earned him a promotion. 他對工作的熱誠奉獻使他獲得了晉升。

Zealot狂熱者，狂熱分子

通常用來形容某人對於特定信仰、政治觀點、或目標持有極端熱情和執著，可能走向極端。

1. The religious zealot was known for his extreme views and actions. 這位宗教狂熱者以他的極端觀點和行動而聞名。

2. The political zealot was willing to do anything to advance his agenda. 這位政治狂熱者願意不擇手段以推進他的議程。

3. Some consider him a zealot, but others admire his unwavering commitment to the cause. 有些人認為他是個狂熱分子，但其他人欽佩他對事業的堅定承諾。

以下是關於這三個詞的一些同義詞：

Zeal（熱情）的同義詞

1. Enthusiasm（熱情）：指對某事物的積極和興奮。
   Her enthusiasm for the project was contagious, inspiring the whole team. 她對這個專案的熱情是具有感染力的，激勵了整個團隊。

2. Passion（激情）：描述對某事物的強烈愛好或熱愛。

3. Fervor（熱情）：形容對某事物的極度熱情和投入。

Zealous（熱情的）的同義詞

1. Eager（渴望的）：指對於某事物急切地渴望或期望。
   He was eager to prove himself in the new job, working long hours to excel. 他渴望在新工作中證明自己，不惜加班以表現優秀。

2. Ardent（熱烈的）：形容對某事物具有強烈的情感和熱情。

3. Devoted（忠誠的）：描述對某事物或目標的忠誠和奉獻。

Zealot（狂熱者）的同義詞

1. Fanatic（狂熱者）：指對於特定信仰、事物或目標有極端熱情的人。

   The political fanatic would stop at nothing to advance his agenda. 這位政治狂熱者不惜一切以推進他的議程。

2. Extremist（極端主義者）：形容持有極端觀點並支持極端行動的人。

3. Radical（激進分子）：描述追求極端改變或行動的個人。

我的日本遊記
——大阪名城天守閣

Today, I visited an important historical and cultural landmark in Japan - the Tenshukaku（天守閣）, also known as the Osaka Castle Keep. It was constructed in 1585 by the prominent figure of Japan's Warring States period（Sengoku Period）, Toyotomi Hideyoshi. The roof is adorned with massive golden beast-head tile ornaments, gleaming in gold and green, while the corridors are embellished with pure gold decorations. The Tenshukaku has become a symbol of Osaka city and showcases the exceptional architectural skills of that era.

After Toyotomi Hideyoshi's passing, the Tenshukaku fell into disrepair. However, Tokugawa Ieyasu, the founder of the Tokugawa Shogunate during Japan's Edo period, inherited Hideyoshi's vision. He undertook the restoration and expansion of the Tenshukaku, making it even more magnificent. Under his leadership, the Tenshukaku became the centerpiece of Edo Castle and a symbol of Tokugawa Ieyasu's prestige and authority. To this day, it remains an important historical and tourist attraction in Japan.

今天我到日本重要的歷史文化和觀光的重要遺跡——天守閣

てんしゅかく（Tenshukaku）參觀，是日本戰國時代的重要人物「豐臣秀吉」1585年興建，屋頂上裝飾著巨大的金色獸頭瓦，金碧輝煌，走廊中還鑲嵌有純金飾品。「天守閣」也成為Osaka城市的象徵，並表現出當時建築技術的精湛。豐臣秀吉逝世後，「天守閣」遭到毀壞，「德川家康」則繼承豐臣秀吉的遺志，完成了豐臣秀吉天守閣的修復和擴建，使其成為更加瑰麗，在他的領導下，天守閣成為江戶城的核心，也成為德川家康威望和權威的象徵，直到今日仍是日本重要的歷史文化和觀光的重要遺跡。

Tokugawa Ieyasu, the founder of the Tokugawa Shogunate, passed away in 1616. He carried on Toyotomi Hideyoshi's legacy by restoring and enhancing the grandeur of the Tenshukaku, turning it into a magnificent architectural marvel. Under his leadership, the Tenshukaku became the heart of Edo Castle and a symbol of Tokugawa Ieyasu's power and influence. It continues to stand as a significant historical and tourist landmark in Tokyo today.

德川家康是日本德川幕府江戶時代的開創者，於1616年去世。他繼承豐臣秀吉的遺志，完成了豐臣秀吉天守閣的修復和擴建，使其成為更加壯麗的建築。在他的領導下，天守閣成為江戶城的核心，也成為德川家康威望和權威的象徵，直到今日仍在東京作為重要的歷史和觀光地標存在。

以下為閱讀文章時需要知道的單字及解釋：
1. Sengoku Period（Warring States period）戰國時期之意

2. Toyotomi Hideyoshi豐臣秀吉：天守閣／てんしゅかく

3. Tenshukaku是日本戰國時代的重要人物「豐臣秀吉」1585年興建

4. Tenshukaku天守閣

5. Fall into disrepair逐漸破敗／荒廢

6. Tokugawa Ieyasu德川家康：德川家康是日本江戶時代的開創者，於1616年去世。他繼承豐臣秀吉的遺志，完成了豐臣秀吉天守閣的修復和擴建。

7. Tokugawa Shogunate德川幕府江戶時期

8. Grandeur輝煌

9. Edo Castle江戶城

10. Embellish裝飾

國家圖書館出版品預行編目資料

Fancy English精湛英文／謝文欽著. --初版.--臺
中市：白象文化事業有限公司，2023.12
　　面；　公分
ISBN 978-626-364-147-1（平裝）
1.CST: 英語 2.CST: 讀本
805.18　　　　　　　　　112016908

Fancy English精湛英文

作　　者　謝文欽
校　　對　謝文欽
發 行 人　張輝潭
出版發行　白象文化事業有限公司
　　　　　412台中市大里區科技路1號8樓之2（台中軟體園區）
　　　　　出版專線：（04）2496-5995　　傳眞：（04）2496-9901
　　　　　401台中市東區和平街228巷44號（經銷部）
　　　　　購書專線：（04）2220-8589　　傳眞：（04）2220-8505
出版編印　林榮威、陳逸儒、黃麗穎、水邊、陳婷婷、李婕、林金郎
設計創意　張禮南、何佳誼
經紀企劃　張輝潭、徐錦淳、林尉儒、張馨方
經銷推廣　李莉吟、莊博亞、劉育姍、林政泓
行銷宣傳　黃姿虹、沈若瑜
營運管理　曾千熏、羅禎琳
印　　刷　基盛印刷工場
初版一刷　2023年12月
定　　價　350元

白象文化
www.ElephantWhite.com.tw

印書小舖
PressStore出版聯網

出版 · 經銷 · 宣傳 · 設計
f 自費出版的領導者　購書 白象文化生活館